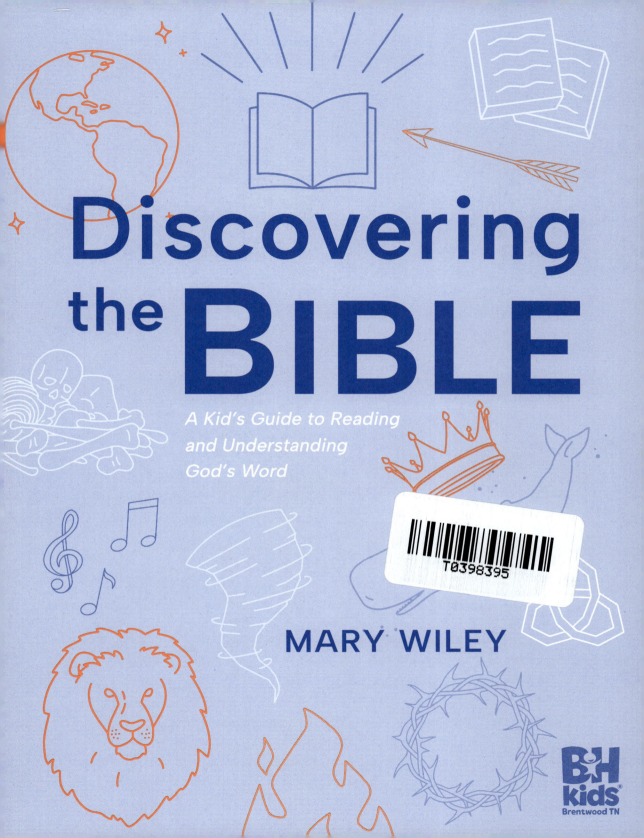

Copyright © 2025 by Mary Wiley
All rights reserved.

Published in 2025 by B&H Publishing Group,
Brentwood, Tennessee.

ISBN: 978-1-4300-8871-4

Scripture quotations are taken from the Christian Standard Bible®,
Copyright © 2017 by Holman Bible Publishers.
Used by permission. Christian Standard Bible® and CSB® are
federally registered trademarks of Holman Bible Publishers.

Dewey Decimal Classification: C220.7
Subject Heading:BIBLE—STUDY AND TEACHING / BIBLE—READING / BIBLE—USE

A special thanks to Jacy Corral (@jacycorral)
for illustrating the icons throughout this book.

Printed in Dongguan, Guangdong, China, November 2024
1 2 3 4 5 6 • 29 28 27 26 25

CONTENTS

INTRODUCTION 4
How to Use This Book 5

THE STORY OF THE BIBLE ... 6
Why Read the Bible? 9
How Is the Bible Organized? ..10
How Do We Study the Bible? ..15

THE LAW 27
Genesis 40
Exodus 41
Leviticus 42
Numbers 43
Deuteronomy 44

HISTORY WRITING 45
Joshua 59
Judges 60
Ruth 61
1 & 2 Samuel 62–63
1 & 2 Kings 64–65
1 & 2 Chronicles 66–67
Ezra 68
Nehemiah 69
Esther 70

WISDOM 71
Job 82
Psalms 83
Proverbs 84
Ecclesiastes 85
Song of Songs 86

THE PROPHETS 87
Isaiah 100
Jeremiah 101
Lamentation 102
Ezekiel 103
Daniel 104
Hosea 106–107
Joel 106–107

Amos 106–107
Obadiah 106–107
Jonah 106–107
Micah 106–107
Nahum 106–107
Habakkuk 106–107
Zephaniah 106–107
Haggai 106–107
Zechariah 106–107
Malachi 106–107

THE GOSPELS AND ACTS .. 109
Matthew 123
Mark 124
Luke 125
John 126
Acts 127

THE LETTERS 129
Romans 140
1 & 2 Corinthians 140
1 & 2 Timothy 140
Titus 140
Philemon 140
Hebrews 140
James 140
1 & 2 Peter 140
1, 2, & 3 John 140
Jude 142

THE APOCALYPTIC WRITING 145
Revelation 155

THROUGH THE BIBLE IN A YEAR 156
365-Day Reading Plan 156
Memory Verses 165
For Teachers and Kid's Ministry Volunteers 166
52 Weeks Through the Bible 168

INTRODUCTION

The Bible is the most important book ever.

The Bible, or God's Word, is unlike any book anyone has ever read. It's alive! This doesn't mean it will stand up and walk across our tables. It means that God speaks to His people through the Bible. We don't just learn about God when we read it; we meet with Him. If you are a Christian, God helps your **mind understand** and your **heart love** the amazing truth found inside the Bible. And you can even talk back through prayer!

This book gives tools to help you read the Bible better and respond in prayer and praise. Any time we read Scripture, God meets with us there. This is the beauty of the Christian life—God has shown us Himself through His Word! We're going to learn and grow together as we learn how to study the Bible.

If this book will help me read the Bible better, does that mean I'm reading it wrong now? The way you read the Bible right now isn't wrong or "broken," but we can always learn how to read and study the Bible better.

HOW TO USE THIS BOOK

This book helps you study the Bible. You can keep it with your Bible so it'll be there any time you need it.

The first section, called "How to Read the Bible," is one you'll come back to often. It tells the story of Scripture, reviews the Bible's organization, explains why we should study the Bible, and gives a four-step guide to use any time we read the Bible called the Start-to-Study guide.

The rest of the book is organized like the Bible is.

The books of the Bible are organized by categories, kind of like different songs are. Some songs are jazz, some are rock, and some are rap. This is called the song's **genre**. Each book of the Bible has a genre too! Genre pages are throughout this book to help you learn all about every book's category. Finally, there is an All-About page for each book of the Bible. These pages are in the same order as the sixty-six books in your copy of God's Word.

So flip through this book and get familiar with where everything is. Then, follow these five steps:

1. **Decide what book of the Bible you'll read.**
2. **Find the Genre page for the book and read it.**
3. **Read about the book in its All-About page.**
4. **Read one of the book's practice passages in your Bible.**
5. **Answer the questions from the Start-to-Study guide on page 17.**

How do I decide what part of the Bible to read?
There are 365 practice passages listed throughout the All-About pages. If you read one every day, you would read many of the important passages from Genesis to Revelation in a year!

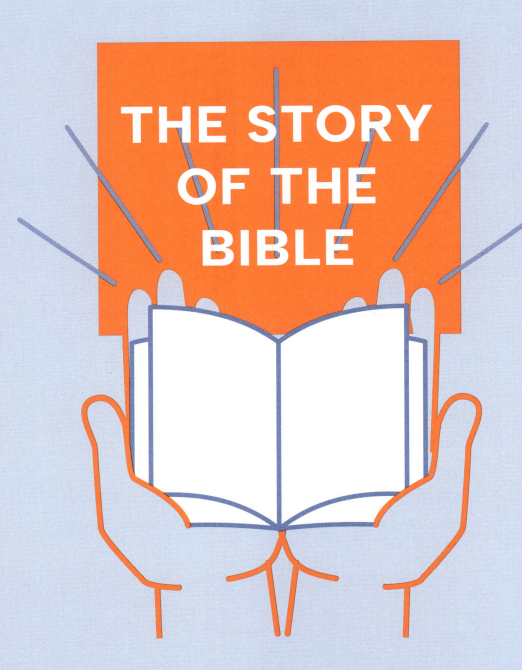

The Bible is one amazing story about God saving His people so that they can be with Him forever through His Son, Jesus Christ.

WHAT'S THE MAIN POINT?

As John said, "But these are written so that you may believe that Jesus is the Messiah, the Son of God, and that by believing you may have life in his name" (John 20:31).

READING BACKWARDS

We read all of the Bible knowing that Jesus is the promised Savior and that He has made a way for us to be made right with God by living a sinless life, dying on the cross, and raising to life again. While the Bible begins with creation and Adam and Eve in the garden, they are not the main characters. While their **sin** comes with consequences, even then, God shows them that He will be with them and will right their wrongs through Jesus.

What is sin? Sin is when our hearts love anything more than God. It causes us to think, do, or say things that are apart from God's good plan for life.

SO THAT WE MAY HAVE LIFE

The ultimate consequence of Adam's sin is death, and only God's Son could bring us back to life in Him. Jesus is called the Second Adam is the Bible. He does what Adam could not do, living perfectly in all of His ways, paying for sin on the cross, and raising from the dead. And if you trust Him, you, too, have been raised from death to life!

PLOT

Have you ever heard your teacher say the word *plot*? Every great story has a beginning, middle, and end. The introduction introduces the most important characters and explains where the story happens. Then, something (usually bad) called a crisis happens to the main characters. The pressure builds until the story reaches a peak, or climax, like climbing a mountain. Then, something else happens (usually good) to release the pressure, and the action falls into a resolution, or an end that makes sense of all that has happened.

This book is not an English class, and the Bible is absolutely not a fictional story. It's true! Still, God is the best author and the story of Scripture follows this plot:

The first five books, known together as the Law, introduce the story. It introduces God and His chosen people. God is the main character in this story, and His people are usually the ones causing crises. God gave His people the Law, but the people chose to disobey it. They did not love and follow God. **The crisis builds throughout the other Old Testament genres.**

The climax in the story is Jesus in the Gospels. God the Son became a human and lived with His people so that they (and we) might know and love God rightly. He paid for His people's sins on the cross, rose from the dead three days later, and ascended to be with God the Father in heaven. This climax is the greatest moment in the Bible—the whole story. It's all about Him.

DON'T MISS THIS: While this storyline is helpful, God's work through Jesus isn't just a moment on a timeline. He has been planning and working to save us since before He created time. His salvation will last forever.

In the falling action, which is the books of Acts and the Letters, God's people were and still are learning to live as new, healed people because of what Jesus did. One day, all will be made right in **the resolution, found in Revelation,** that God has promised: eternal life with Him for all who love Him and trust Jesus as their Savior.

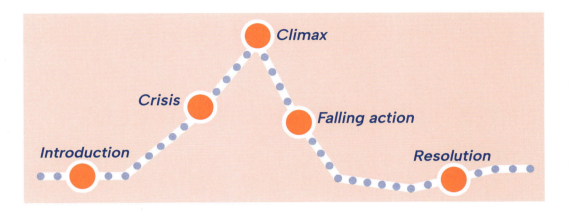

WHY READ THE BIBLE?

Have you ever read the Bible and wondered what was going on?

The Bible can be hard to read. There are words you've never seen before and stories that don't make sense because of the differences between your life and the lives of the people in the stories. We don't live in the same places or know the same things as the writers of the Bible.

But it wasn't only people writing the words of the Bible. The Holy Spirit guided the writers to write and made sure there were no mistakes in God's Word. And the Holy Spirit who guided them now helps us understand what they wrote. God's Word was not just meaningful for those living in Bible times; it also is meaningful for us today, even if we don't always understand all the details. The Bible is always good for *all* people at *all* times in *all* places. **We read the Bible because we want to know God better.**

What can I do to understand the parts of the Bible that are confusing? First, pray and ask the Holy Spirit to help you understand. Next, use resources (like this one!) or ask someone else to teach you what the writers meant.

HOW IS THE BIBLE ORGANIZED?

There are sixty-six books in the Bible that tell the amazing story of who God is and how He gives people life. (You can read all about it on the Story of the Bible and Plot pages.) But those sixty-six books don't tell the story in the exact order.

Instead, the Bible is organized into categories, or genres: Law, History, Wisdom, Prophets, Gospels and Acts, Letters, and Apocalyptic. In the same way we read a short story differently than we read the news, a poem, or a book of facts about sharks, the genres in the Bible help us read and understand each book better.

GENRES

LAW: This genre describes the character of the Law-Giver and the promise of the Savior to God's people. The Law includes the first five books of the Bible.

HISTORY: Books in the History genre tell about events in the life of God's people, and they show us how Jesus fulfills those happenings if we are reading rightly. The books between Joshua and Esther in your Bible are all in the History genre.

WISDOM: Wisdom writings include Job, Psalms, Proverbs, Ecclesiastes, and Song of Songs. These books teach the reader how to live a wise life in the world, which is to live like Jesus, who is often described as Wisdom in the Bible.

PROPHETS: God used prophets to warn people whose hearts were far from God to turn away from their disobedience and follow God. Jesus is the Promised One who brings justice in the Prophets. There are seventeen total books in this genre.

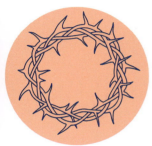

GOSPELS AND ACTS: Matthew, Mark, Luke, and John tell the story of Jesus's life, death, resurrection, and ascension. These four books tell the same story in different ways because each writer had the goal of telling the good news about Jesus *to different people* in *different ways*. Acts tells the story of what follows the good news of Jesus: the beginning of the church.

LETTERS: All of the letters in the Bible (except Hebrews) were written by the apostles Paul, Peter, James, and John, who sent letters to churches, friends, and missionaries. We don't know who wrote Hebrews, but we do know that God intended for us to read it! Most letters share a specific reason that they were written (we call this an *occasion*). The letters encouraged the early church in the time period soon after Jesus ascended to heaven.

APOCALYPTIC: Revelation is the only book that is in the apocalyptic genre, although parts of other books, like Daniel, also include this type of writing. Apocalyptic writing normally includes an author's vision of what will happen when Jesus returns and we live with Him forever. This type of writing has lots of symbols, allegories, and metaphors, which the writer rarely explains.

BOOKS OF THE BIBLE BY GENRE

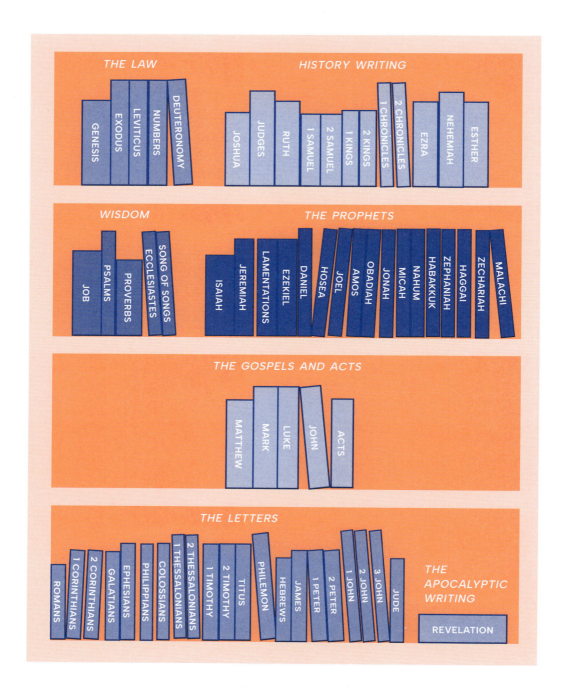

SUBGENRES

As you read, you'll often find different categories of writing inside each book. A book of the Law, like Genesis, may have laws, genealogies, narratives, and poetry, while the Gospels have parables, sermons, and narratives. Below are the subgenres (the genres within other genres) you'll read in the Bible most often.

ALLUSION is when the author mentions another part of Scripture. Sometimes this won't be obvious, because the author might not tell you they are pointing to other verses. *Example: Hebrews 11*

APOCALYPTIC WRITING normally includes an author's vision of the end times. While Revelation is the only full book of apocalyptic writing, others have this type of writing as a subgenre. *Examples: Isaiah 24–27; 33; Daniel 7–12*

GENEALOGIES (sometimes also called census) are a list of family members from the male side of the family. *Example: Matthew 1:1–17*

NARRATIVES tell what happened. They don't include every detail but what the author thought was important. When we read the story of Cain killing Abel, it describes what happened, not how we should live. *Example: Genesis 4*

PARABLES are stories that teach important lessons. The story may be a true event, detailing something that happened, or it may be fiction. Parables always teach timeless wisdom to the listener. *Examples: Judges 9:7–15; Matthew 13:24–30*

POETRY AND SONG use rhyme or other beautiful ways to talk about an idea. This subgenre can include repetition, contrast (how things are different), comparison (how things are similar), hyperbole (exaggeration for emphasis), or personification (assigning non-living things human attributes). *Examples: Exodus 15; Psalm 1; Psalm 98:8*

PROPHECY is a promise of something to come or an interpretation of what is currently happening. These promises are often delivered by a messenger of God, but they can be delivered by God Himself. Prophecy is often about upcoming judgment and calls the hearers to repent. There are entire books of prophecy and prophecies within other genres. *Examples: 1 Kings 16:1–7; Daniel 7*

PROVERBS are statements of truth, often spoken by wise teachers. They advise how to live a good life. They should be read as generally good rules to follow for wise living, not promises that will be fulfilled. *Examples: Proverbs 3:7–8; Proverbs 10:3*

SERMONS are longer passages where only one person is talking. They are teaching something true about God. *Example: Deuteronomy 30*

TYPOLOGY occurs when a person in the Bible foreshadows what Jesus will be like or not like. These people are flawed and are not Jesus, but they still show us something of what Jesus is like. *Examples: Genesis 37–50; Jonah*

HOW DO WE STUDY THE BIBLE?

Studying the Bible—reading it carefully and thinking deeply about it—is all about knowing God. We study the Bible so that we can know God more. Here are four steps to study the Bible each time you read it:

> 1. PRAY
> 2. READ AND REREAD
> 3. ASK AND ANSWER
> 4. RESPOND AND PRAY AGAIN

Page 17 includes a blank worksheet called a **Start-to-Study guide**. You can draw it on a piece of paper or in a notebook where you keep all your Bible-reading notes. The worksheet is blank so that you'll always have a copy you can use as a guide.

1. PRAY. Ask God to help you understand as you read.

2. READ AND REREAD. Read the passage more than once.

3. ASK AND ANSWER. First, summarize what you read in one sentence or act it out, draw a picture, or write a song. If the passage tells about something that happened, try writing or drawing it on a timeline.

ASK as many questions as you can about what you read.

- Who? What? When? Where? Why?
- What word or phrase don't I understand?
- What's happening in this paragraph? Chapter? Book?
- Is anything repeated?
- What is this passage teaching me about God and the good news of Jesus?
- What does this passage show me about people?
- Is it describing something that happened? Or is it telling me how to live?
- What else am I curious about?

ANSWER those questions if you can. Read the verses nearby to see if they help. If your Bible has cross-references (other verses in the margins of the page) or study notes, read them. If you still have unanswered questions, ask a parent or leader.

4. RESPOND AND PRAY AGAIN. After you have read and reread the passage and asked and answered as many questions as you can, you should respond to what you read. You can pray and thank God for what you learned about Him, listen to worship music, or ask God to help your love for Him and for others to grow. Write your prayer down on your paper.

If I could only ask one question about the passage, what should it be? Probably "What does this passage teach me about God?" The Bible is a book about God, who shows us Himself through the words on the Bible's pages. He's the One we worship, so we want to know Him better every time we read.

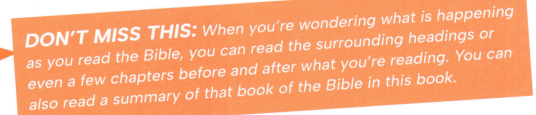

DON'T MISS THIS: When you're wondering what is happening as you read the Bible, you can read the surrounding headings or even a few chapters before and after what you're reading. You can also read a summary of that book of the Bible in this book.

Passage: Scripture verse

START-TO-STUDY

1. PRAY
2. READ AND REREAD

Date: Today

SUMMARIZE OR DRAW A PICTURE OF WHAT YOU READ:

3. ASK AND ANSWER *Review pages 15 & 16 for help with what to ask.*

ASK:	ANSWER:
1. Who? What? When? Where? Why?	1.
2. What is God showing me about Himself?	2.
3. What is God showing me about people?	3.

4. RESPOND AND PRAY *Write a prayer thanking God for what you learned about Him. Ask God to help you worship Him.*

GO DEEPER

As you start using the Start-to-Study guide to help you read the Bible, you'll get better and better at praying, reading, asking, and responding. When you're ready for a deeper challenge, you can begin to learn about genre, discover the main idea and key images of each passage, and choose a verse to memorize. Copy the Start-to-Study: Go Deeper worksheet from page 22 on your paper so we can practice together.

NAME THE GENRE

Remember, the Bible is organized by genre. So is this book! Flip to the All-About page for the book of the Bible you are reading and write down the genre on your paper. Then read the Genre pages that explain what the genre is and how to read it well.

Check out pages 10-14 for a refresher of the genres!

Let's practice together. If you were reading Proverbs 1, what genre would you write on your sheet? Go find Proverbs in this book—it's near the middle. Proverbs is in the Wisdom genre, so you would write "Wisdom" on your paper and then read pages 81-86 to learn more about that genre.

At the end of each genre, you'll find questions to ask. Write those questions in the *Key Questions to Ask and Answer for This Genre* section. Answer them from the passage you read.

DISCOVER THE MAIN IDEA

What is the main idea of the passage? It's the most important part! Often, the main ideas are repeated. Sometimes, other points follow the main one to make it stronger (as if the author is trying to win an argument). Summarize the main idea in a sentence.

LET'S PRACTICE TOGETHER. Read Proverbs 1, and write down the main idea in a sentence.

_____

_____

_____

_____

MEMORIZE

Choose any verse from the passage to memorize. On each book's All-About page, you'll find suggested verses to memorize, but you can choose any verse!

Here are some ideas to help you memorize:

1. Write the verse on an index card and take it wherever you go.

2. Jot it on a card, put it in a plastic sandwich bag, and tape it to your shower's wall so you can review it every day.

3. Make up a tune and sing the verse.

4. Create motions to help you remember each word.

LET'S PRACTICE TOGETHER. Choose a verse from Proverbs 1 and try to memorize it. Write it down in the Memorize section of your guide. Memorizing God's Word gives you tools to respond with truth to hard times in your life.

Passage: **START-TO-STUDY** *Date:*
Scripture verse **GO DEEPER** Today

GENRE:

KEY QUESTIONS TO ASK AND ANSWER FOR THIS GENRE:

ASK:	**ANSWER:**
1.	1.

MAIN IDEA:

KEY IMAGES: *Mark the ones that apply.*

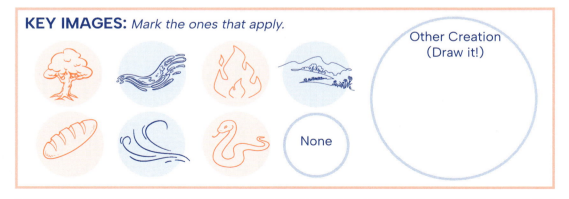

MEMORIZE:

A FEW IMPORTANT NOTES ABOUT BIBLE READING

NO SECRET CODES
There is no special way of reading that will "unlock" a hidden truth or secret meaning. We don't need to do math or decode messages. We read what the Bible *actually says* instead of what we want it to say. Studying the Bible and its genres will help us understand what the author wanted readers to know.

NO WARM FUZZY FEELINGS EVERY TIME
The Bible isn't a magical book of feel-good stories; it is an invitation to meet with God. Sometimes, you'll read something like Leviticus and wonder why there are so many laws and details. The good news of the Bible is amazing, but the goal of your reading is not to find one warm, fuzzy truth. It's to meet with God and let Him change your heart as you read.

NOT JUST INSTRUCTIONS
The Bible is not just instructions for a good life with God. It does include lots of instructions, but God gave us the Bible so that we can get to know and love Him as we read—not so we can be on our best behavior.

IT'S ALL ABOUT JESUS
Jesus isn't only in the New Testament! You can find reminders of Jesus throughout the whole Bible—from the very first chapter. The Bible shows us Jesus and the good news of Jesus's perfect life, sacrificial death, resurrection, and ascension. Jesus shows us God because He is God—and because of Jesus, we can know and love God forever.

FIND KEY IMAGES

Word pictures explain what God is like, what it looks like to grow spiritually and how we connect with God. Although word pictures won't be in every passage you read, several word pictures are used throughout the whole Bible! When you see one, ask, *"What is God showing me about Himself?"*

TREES: The Bible starts with two trees in the garden of Eden and ends with a tree in the center of the new creation. You can keep a **green** colored pencil nearby as you study the Bible so that you can underline when trees are mentioned.

WATER: At creation, the Bible says the Spirit hovered over water, preparing it for life. God provides water from a rock in the wilderness, and the waters of the Jordan must be crossed to enter the Promised Land. When Jesus dies on the cross, water comes from His side. Underline water in your Bible with a **blue** colored pencil.

FIRE: God appears to Moses in a burning bush, leads His people through the wilderness in a pillar of fire, and commands that sacrifices be burned on the altar in the tabernacle. Keep an **orange** colored pencil nearby and underline fire anytime you see it.

LAND: God placed Adam and Eve in a specific land, the garden of Eden. It was their home. Then, He rescued His people out of a land that was not theirs and took them to the Promised Land. Land matters in the Bible. Underline the word with a **brown** colored pencil.

BREAD: Unleavened bread is a big part of the Passover meal, the word *Jerusalem* means "the house of bread," and Jesus calls Himself the bread of life. Use a **yellow** colored pencil to underline bread.

WIND: God spoke to Job in a whirlwind. When the Holy Spirit came to those who followed Jesus after He ascended to heaven, people heard the sound of a rushing wind. When wind is mentioned in Scripture, underline it in **purple**.

SERPENT: A serpent spoke to Eve in the garden, and it was a royal symbol worn by the pharaohs in Egypt. God also used a serpent to punish the Israelites who complained in the wilderness. Underline serpent with a **red** colored pencil.

Can you think of any other word pictures in the Bible?

PRACTICE

Below is an example of how to use the Start-to-Study guide. Open your Bible to Genesis 1:26–31 and follow along. You'll see how this passage could be marked in the Bible. Repeated ideas are highlighted in orange. Verses 30–31 have a lot of repetition from earlier verses. (This is why it's important to review what's a little before and a little after each passage.)

---

1. READ AND REREAD Genesis 1:26–31.

²⁶ Then God said, "Let us make man in our image, according to our likeness. They will rule the fish of the sea, the birds of the sky, the livestock, the whole earth, and the creatures that crawl on the earth."

²⁷ So God created man
in his own image;
he created him in the image of God;
he created them male and female.

²⁸ God blessed them, and God said to them, "Be fruitful, multiply, fill the earth, and subdue it. Rule the fish of the sea, the birds of the sky, and every creature that crawls on the earth." ²⁹ God also said, "Look, I have given you every seed-bearing plant on the surface of the entire earth and every tree whose fruit contains seed. This will be food for you, ³⁰ for all the wildlife of the earth, for every bird of the sky, and for every creature that crawls on the earth—everything having the breath of life in it—I have given every green plant for food." And it was so. ³¹ God saw all that he had made, and it was very good indeed. Evening came and then morning: the sixth day.

Passage: Genesis 1:26-31

START-TO-STUDY

Date: Today

1. **PRAY**
2. **READ AND REREAD**

SUMMARIZE OR DRAW A PICTURE OF WHAT YOU READ:

God made people in His image and gave them a job to fill the earth with more people and to take care of it. He said everything He made was very good!

3. ASK AND ANSWER *Review pages 17 & 18 for help with what to ask.*

ASK:

1. What does it mean that we are made in God's image and likeness?
2. Why were the people God made "very good indeed" when the rest of what He created was just "good" (from earlier in Genesis 1)?
3. When did this happen?
4. Who were these people?
5. What did God tell Adam and Eve to do?
6. What does this instruction mean?
7. How did God create man?

ANSWER:

1. We show what God is like in some ways and are valuable because of this.
2. God loves people! We are His best creation, because people are like Him.
3. On the sixth day of creation.
4. Adam and Eve (Genesis 2).
5. To be fruitful and multiply.
6. Rule creation, have children, and do good work that helps others and the rest of creation.
7. Genesis 2:7 shows us that God made Adam from the dust.

4. RESPOND AND PRAY *Write a prayer thanking God for what you learned about Him. Ask God to help you worship Him.*

God, You are powerful over all things. Thank You for being the good Creator of everything. Thank You for creating me in Your image and showing me how much You love me! Please help me be a good example of what it looks like to follow You with all the people around me. Help me see people the way You see them. In Jesus's name, amen.

Passage: Genesis 1:26-31

START-TO-STUDY
GO DEEPER

Date: Today

GENRE: Law

KEY QUESTIONS TO ASK AND ANSWER FOR THIS GENRE:

ASK:
1. What is the Law-Giver like?
2. Where do I see God keeping His promises?
3. How does this passage show the effects of sin?
4. How should I live because of what is true about God's character?

ANSWER:
1. God is Creator.
2. God hadn't made promises to His people yet because they were just being created.
3. Sin wasn't in the world yet.
4. God is powerful and rules over all. I can praise Him for His power and obey Him as Ruler.

MAIN IDEA:
God created men and women. God loves us dearly and gives us good work to do.

KEY IMAGES: *Mark the ones that apply.*

[✓ tree] [water] [fire] [mountains] [Other Creation (Draw it!)]
[bread] [waves] [snake] [None]

MEMORIZE: Genesis 1:27: So God created man in his own image; he created him in the image of God; he created them male and female.

GENRE: LAW

THE LAW includes the first five books of the Bible. It tells the story of God's people: creation, the fall, God's calling of His people, their slavery in Egypt, and wandering in the wilderness before they went into Canaan, God's Promised Land.

- **Genesis** reveals that God created everything and is powerful.
- **Exodus** shows that God dearly loves and rescues His people.
- **Leviticus**, **Numbers**, and **Deuteronomy** are where God gives His instructions so that we know everything it takes to live the good life God designed for His people.

The Law also tells **the story of the beginning of time and the origin story of God's chosen people**. He made covenants—or promises—with Adam, Noah, Abraham, Isaac, Jacob, Moses, and Aaron, which would be fulfilled in Jesus. God promised to

1. always be their God,
2. make them a large nation,
3. and give them land to live in where He would be with them forever.

God's people faced many hard things before they made it to His Promised Land in Canaan. They were slaves in Egypt for more than 400 years. They wandered in the wilderness between Egypt and Canaan for forty years. Almost no one who left Egypt got to enter the Promised Land, because they did not trust God. Even Moses did not get to go because of his disbelief. The Law closes just before His people went into the land God had prepared for them. Moses died and was buried by God in the land of Moab, which had to happen before they could go into the land.

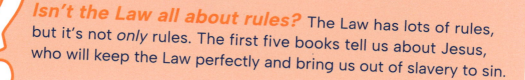

Isn't the Law all about rules? The Law has lots of rules, but it's not *only* rules. The first five books tell us about Jesus, who will keep the Law perfectly and bring us out of slavery to sin.

The first five books **help us understand everything else in the Bible**. They teach us who God is, what He is like, and why we need Him.

WHERE ARE WE IN THE STORY?

The law is the introduction of the story. It tells us who God is, who His people are, and what He is like.

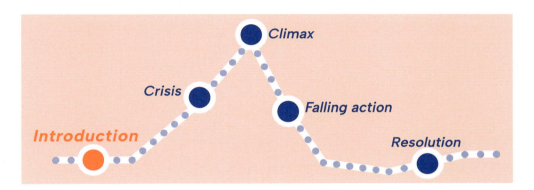

HOW TO READ THE LAW

The Law is an introduction to everything else that happens in the Bible. You can read it as the foundation of the story God wrote for us. **Look for what is true about God as the Law-Giver.** He is introducing *Himself* to us through everything written in these books.

THE GOSPEL STORY IN THE LAW

God is the Creator of all things, and all of creation and all of His ways are good. In the first few verses of Genesis He shows us that He is Trinity: Father, Son, and Spirit. The **Father** is the giver of all good gifts. He speaks to, guides, and shows His great love to His people throughout the books of the Law. In Genesis 1:2, the **Spirit** is hovering over the water. Colossians 1:16 also tells us that God created all things through His Word, who is identified as His **Son** in John 1.

When Adam sinned, death was the consequence. Their bodies didn't die immediately, but they were spiritually dead because they had to be separated from God, the source of life. Yet God was not surprised. He had already planned for Jesus to come (Genesis 3:15).

God is a good Law-Giver. He gives rules that help people, but people don't always want to obey those rules. While there were and are consequences for disobedience, God continued to show kindness to His people. He promised to rescue them, and He did. He brought them to the Promised Land. Ultimately, the origin story of God's people in the Law points to an even bigger promise God kept: providing salvation for His people through Jesus.

MAIN POINTS OF THE LAW

1. God is always good.

Everything God creates and instructs is good because *God is always good*. Throughout the Law, God is with His people, helping and providing for them.

2. Sin leads to death.

The consequence of sin in the garden of Eden was *death for all*. In the five books of the Law, God helps His people know that they need to be made right with Him.

3. God keeps His promises.

God makes and keeps covenants. Even when people don't keep their side of the covenant, *God always keeps His promises*.

KEY IMAGES

Water

The Spirit hovers over the water at creation, the flood destroys the earth, God's people cross the Red Sea and, later, the Jordan. Each time water is mentioned, God is doing something new.

Land

Land is important throughout the Bible. God promises land in His covenants and leads His people to it.

Serpent

There are several **serpents** in the Law (like in Genesis 3 and Numbers 21:4–9). Serpents were often considered to be a sign of wisdom or power. As you read about serpents, pay attention to when that wisdom is good and when it is bad.

WHERE WAS THIS HAPPENING & WHAT WAS GOING ON IN THE WORLD?

The books of the Law took place in the Middle East and Northern Africa. As the world began and the population grew, groups of people, called tribes, lived in the area where God's people were. Battles, wars, and people being captured and taken to another nation as exiles were commonplace. Most nations worshiped false gods. The Law includes lots of rules that seem strange to us today, but they are important. They kept God's people from following false gods unlike the peoples around them.

THINGS YOU NEED TO KNOW
COVENANTS

In the Law, God makes **covenants** with His people.

Covenant	Key Text	Key Promise
Adam	Genesis 1:26–30 and 2:16–17; Genesis 3:14–19	In Genesis 1, God gave people the garden to cultivate. Their only rule was to not eat from the tree of the knowledge of good and evil. They did not obey this rule and faced the consequence of death for their disobedience. Still, God promised a Rescuer would come and crush the head of the serpent.
Noah	Genesis 9:8–11	God promised He would never destroy the earth with a flood again.
Abraham, Isaac, and Jacob	Genesis 15; 17:1–14	God promised to make Abraham and his children a large, great nation that would be a blessing to other nations around them. Abraham's family was told to circumcise their boys and men as a sign of being in God's family.
Moses	Exodus 19:3–6	God promised His people He would treasure them and that they would become "[his] kingdom of priests and [his] holy nation" (Exodus 19:6).
The Priests	Numbers 25:12–13	God made a covenant of peace with the descendants of Aaron. They would have a lasting priesthood.

DON'T MISS THIS: Covenants began in the Law, but they are given later too. God made a covenant with David in 2 Samuel 7:12–16. And the new covenant (Jeremiah 31:31–34) that God has established through Jesus is available to all who trust Him. God is a promise-making, promise-keeping God!

THE JOURNEY OF THE LAW

Exodus, Leviticus, Numbers, and Deuteronomy all take place in the wilderness. God's people left Egypt and wandered in the wilderness, stopping at Mount Sinai for a year to receive the Law. When they came to Kadesh–Barnea, they sent twelve spies into the Promised Land.

THE ROUTE OF THE EXODUS

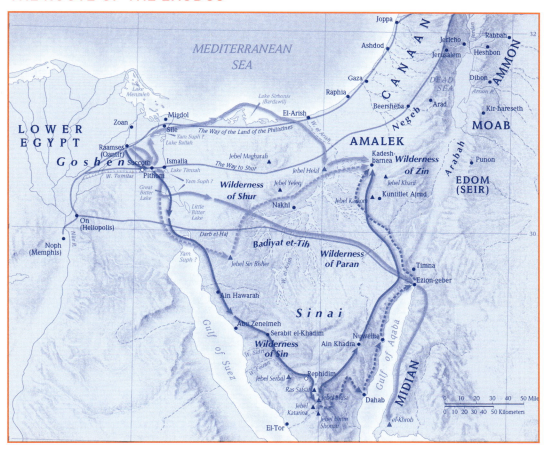

It would have been pretty easy for God's people to continue walking north and enter Canaan, the Promised Land. But God's people were afraid. They didn't trust God would give them the land as He said He would. Their punishment was forty years of wandering.

The journey from Kadesh–Barnea began in Deuteronomy 1. By Deuteronomy 34, the journey had taken God's people to Moab, where they were just before they crossed the Jordan River into the Promised Land. Here's what that journey could have looked like:

THE JOURNEY FROM KADESH–BARNEA TO THE PLAINS OF MOAB

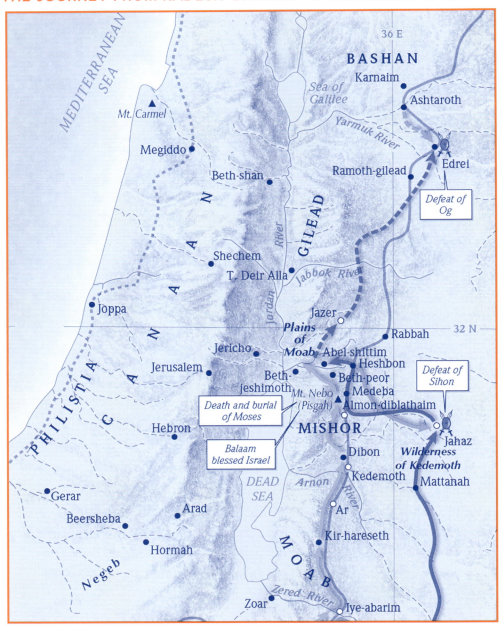

KEY QUESTIONS TO ASK & ANSWER WHEN READING THE LAW

1. What is the Law-Giver like?
2. Where do I see God keeping His promises?
3. How does this passage show the effects of sin?
4. How should I live because of what is true about God's character?

If you can't answer a question from a passage you read, don't worry! Just write that the passage doesn't answer it and keep going. Not every question will be answered by every passage.

PRACTICE IN THE LAW

GENESIS
1. Genesis 1
2. Genesis 3
3. Genesis 7:1–10; 8:1–4
4. Genesis 9:1–17
5. Genesis 11:1–9
6. Genesis 12
7. Genesis 15
8. Genesis 21:1–7; 22:1–19
9. Genesis 28:10–22; 32:24–32
10. Genesis 37; 41–42

EXODUS
11. Exodus 1:1–14
12. Exodus 3:1–22
13. Exodus 6:2–13
14. Exodus 11–12
15. Exodus 14:5–31
16. Exodus 19–20:17
17. Exodus 25:1–9
18. Exodus 32:1–35
19. Exodus 33:12–23
20. Exodus 34:1–14

LEVITICUS
21. Leviticus 5:1–6
22. Leviticus 9:22–24
23. Leviticus 10:1–3
24. Leviticus 16:1–34
25. Leviticus 20:22–26
26. Leviticus 26:1–46

NUMBERS
27. Numbers 3:1–13
28. Numbers 3:40–51
29. Numbers 7:1–5, 89
30. Numbers 9:1–23
31. Numbers 13:1–33
32. Numbers 14:1–38
33. Numbers 16:1–35
34. Numbers 21:4–9

DEUTERONOMY
35. Deuteronomy 3:21–29
36. Deuteronomy 4:1–14
37. Deuteronomy 5:1–24
38. Deuteronomy 6:4–8
39. Deuteronomy 8:1–20
40. Deuteronomy 16:1–17
41. Deuteronomy 26:16–19
42. Deuteronomy 29:1–29
43. Deuteronomy 31:1–23
44. Deuteronomy 34:1–12

Passage: Genesis 12:1-9

START-TO-STUDY

Date: Today

1. **PRAY**
2. **READ AND REREAD**

SUMMARIZE OR DRAW A PICTURE OF WHAT YOU READ:

God spoke to Abram and asked him to go to a new land where God would make him into a great nation. Abram obeyed immediately and even built altars to the Lord as he traveled.

---

3. ASK AND ANSWER *Review pages 17 & 18 for help with what to ask.*

ASK:

1. Where was Abram's land?
2. Would it be hard for him to leave?
3. Did God make Abram into a great nation?
4. Who was Lot?
5. How far were they going?
6. What was Abram's seventy-five years like before this?
7. What's so great about the oak of Mamre?
8. How did Abram's wife feel about the move?
9. Why did God give Abram the land?

ANSWER:

1. Ur (Genesis 15:7)
2. Seems like it'd be sad.
3. It doesn't say, but God keeps His promises, so probably yes.
4. Abram's nephew (Genesis 14:12).
5. FAR.
6. Doesn't say.
7. Maybe it'll say later.
8. I wouldn't like it if I was her.
9. Because He chose him and He loved him.

---

4. RESPOND AND PRAY *Write a prayer thanking God for what you learned about Him. Ask God to help you worship Him.*

God, help me tell people in my life the good news about Jesus. Help me hear You and obey You immediately, like Abram did. Thanks for showing me that You love people so much You'd give them a land and choose to be their God. In Jesus's name, amen.

Passage: Genesis 12:1-9

START-TO-STUDY
GO DEEPER

Date: Today

GENRE: Law

KEY QUESTIONS TO ASK AND ANSWER FOR THIS GENRE:

ASK:	ANSWER:
1. What is the Law-Giver like?	1. He chooses people and makes them a great nation.
2. Where do I see God keeping His promises?	2. He would make Abram a great nation and give him lots of kids.
3. How does this passage show the effects of sin?	3. Sin separated us from God. He wouldn't need to send us to His Promised Land; we'd already be with him forever if sin had not come into the world.
4. How should I live because of what is true about God's character?	4. I should obey when God asks me to do something.

MAIN IDEA: God sent Abram and Sarai as His chosen family so that they could know and love God and bless others with the good news that God can be known and loved, because He knows and loves all people.

KEY IMAGES: Mark the ones that apply.

    Other Creation (Draw it!)

  None

MEMORIZE: Genesis 12:1-3: The LORD said to Abram: Go from your land, your relatives, and your father's house to the land that I will show you. I will make you into a great nation, I will bless you, I will make your name great, and you will be a blessing. I will bless those who bless you, I will curse anyone who treats you with contempt, and all the peoples on earth will be blessed through you.

ALL ABOUT THE BOOKS OF THE LAW

GENESIS

Genesis means "beginning." This book tells us about the beginning of *God's world*, the beginning of *sin in the world*, and the beginning of *God's chosen people*.

The first people, Adam and Eve, were made in God's image and placed in a garden. They failed to obey God's instruction and faced consequences. They had to leave the garden, but they didn't go alone. God went with them. God showed His great love for them by making good covenants (or promises) with them, beginning with Adam and Noah, and then Abraham, Isaac, and Jacob. God protected His people from famine (when there's not enough food in the land) by setting Joseph, Jacob's son, as a wise leader in Egypt who could give them food. Jacob's family—God's covenant people—moved to Egypt toward the end of this book.

Genesis is part of the Law because it begins the story of the good Law-Giver who gives rules for the good of His people. It's the rule that is broken that sets the stage for the coming Messiah who will crush the head of the serpent (Genesis 3:15).

WHO?	Moses
WHEN?	Probably the 15th or 14th century BC
WHERE?	From the garden of Eden out into the world around it
SUBGENRES	Narrative, poetry, census, and speeches
VERSES TO MEMORIZE	Genesis 1:1; 1:26–28; 3:21; 12:1–3

EXODUS

God's people were living in Egypt at the end of Genesis. In Exodus, a new pharaoh began to rule Egypt. He did not know of Joseph's wisdom during the famine, so he made God's people slaves. Their slavery lasted 400 years.

God used a man named Moses to rescue His people, and He showed His amazing power by sending ten plagues to convince Pharaoh to let His people go. God's people crossed the Red Sea and entered the wilderness, where God taught them how to be His people by giving them good laws to obey. He also told them to set up a tabernacle where He would meet with them. (In some ways, the tabernacle was like the garden of Eden.) As they wandered in the wilderness, God traveled with them by a pillar of fire or cloud and in the tabernacle.

Exodus includes the laws God gave Moses and the people. These laws began with God, reminding His people that He was the God who saved them from Egypt (Exodus 20:1–2). The Law was never just to tell people what to do. God wanted His people to follow it because God wanted good things for them. Every instruction was because of God's great love for His people.

WHO?	Moses
WHEN?	Probably the 15th or 14th century BC
WHERE?	From Egypt to the wilderness
SUBGENRES	Narrative, poetry, and speeches
VERSES TO MEMORIZE	Exodus 3:14; 14:14; 20:1–2

LEVITICUS

Leviticus reveals the way to life—loving and obeying God—and the way to death—choosing our way and disobeying God. God gave more than 600 laws to help His people live in the "best" way with Him. These laws helped God's people love God above all else, love their neighbors well, make good decisions, and look different from the nations around them. They also showed God's people that on their own, they could never keep all God's laws. Neither can we. We can't live the "best" way with God because we can't keep every rule.

Leviticus also gives instructions for certain people who worked in the tabernacle so that they could meet with God. These men were from the tribe of Levi, which is why the book is called *Leviticus*. Levites made sacrifices for all the people so that they could have a right relationship with God. These sacrifices were made again and again, because the blood of goats or lambs couldn't *actually* cover sin. One day, God's Son would come, perfectly keep God's law, and end the need for sacrifices. His blood would cover our sin and set us free forever. Anyone who trusts in Jesus will be judged as though he or she perfectly kept the Law—because Jesus did it for us.

WHO?	Moses
WHEN?	Probably the 15th or 14th century BC
WHERE?	In the wilderness
SUBGENRES	Narrative, laws
VERSE TO MEMORIZE	Leviticus 20:26

NUMBERS

The book of Numbers records how God provided for and helped His people while they wandered in the wilderness. Numbers is like the second part of the story that began in Exodus. God's people were still in the wilderness during their forty-year journey to the Promised Land. At the beginning of the book, twelve spies went into the Promised Land, but they all returned scared, except for Caleb and Joshua.

Since the people didn't trust God, God sent them back into the wilderness until the entire generation of people, with the exception of Caleb and Joshua, who did not trust God died. God told Moses to take a census, or count the people, in the wilderness two different times: in chapter 1 and in chapter 26. This is why the book is called Numbers.

God expands some of the laws from Leviticus in this book, but most of the book is about the journey of God's people in the wilderness. This book again reveals the character of the Law-Giver. God is merciful and kind, even when His people do not obey Him. He also disciplines them, giving them consequences to remind them of His power and His instruction.

WHO?	Moses
WHEN?	Probably the 15th or 14th century BC
WHERE?	In the wilderness
SUBGENRES	Census and narrative
VERSES TO MEMORIZE	Numbers 6:24–26; 14:18

DEUTERONOMY

Deuteronomy will seem familiar. Deuteronomy means "Second Law," and it repeats much of Exodus and Leviticus. God's people had almost finished wandering in the wilderness and were soon to cross the Jordan into the Promised Land. But most of the people who had received the Law the first time at Mount Sinai had died during the wandering, because they hadn't believed God would keep His promise and give them the land.

A new group of people was born to God's people in the wilderness. This new group would cross the Jordan soon, entering the Promised Land and setting up a nation led by God. They needed to be reminded of God's laws so that they would be different from the nations living in Canaan and wouldn't turn to false gods.

Moses delivered this second law in three sermons (or speeches), reminding the people of all they'd been taught. At the end of the book, the people got ready to cross the Jordan River. God led Moses, who could not go into the Promised Land, to Mount Nebo, where he died. In God's great kindness, God Himself buried Moses there.

WHO?	Moses and Joshua
WHEN?	Probably the 15th or 14th century BC
WHERE?	In the wilderness
SUBGENRES	Sermons, narrative, and laws
VERSE TO MEMORIZE	Deuteronomy 6:4–6

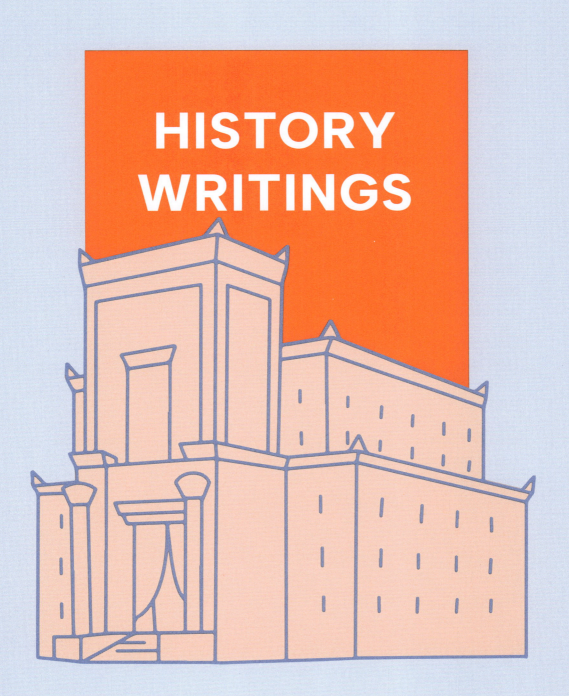
HISTORY WRITINGS

GENRE: HISTORY

THE HISTORY WRITINGS tell the story—or *history*—of God's people. History writings include:

- Joshua
- Judges
- Ruth
- 1 & 2 Samuel
- 1 & 2 Kings
- 1 & 2 Chronicles
- Ezra
- Nehemiah
- Esther

These books tell the history of God's people from when they entered the Promised Land to when they were led by judges and then kings and, finally, to when their kingdom split in two. Throughout this time, God's people sometimes obeyed Him, but usually, they went completely against God and His commands.

God sent **prophets** to call people to come back to Him and obey Him again. Sometimes they responded by turning away from their sin and trusting God. Other times, they continued to sin, or as the Bible says, *do whatever was right in their own eyes*.

God disciplined His people. Other nations exiled God's people. The Assyrians exiled the people of Israel around 722 BC, the Babylonians exiled the people of Judah around 586 BC, and the temple—the place where God's people were supposed to meet with Him—was destroyed.

Eventually, the Persian King Cyrus let God's people go back to the Promised Land. Jerusalem and the temple were destroyed, but some of God's people decided to rebuild the city's walls and the temple so that the people could worship the one true God.

What is exile? At this point in history, exile means being taken from one's home and made to live as a worker in a different place.

WHERE ARE WE IN THE STORY?

The book of Judges says, "Everyone did whatever seemed right to him" (Judges 17:6). This is the crisis: God's people chose to turn away from Him and toward sin, over and over again.

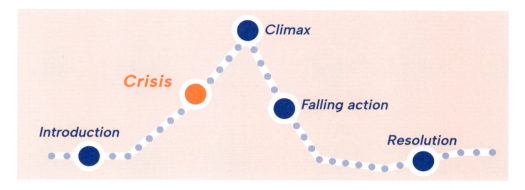

HOW TO READ HISTORY WRITINGS

The History books are written like a story, and that's how you should read them. Remember, writers during Bible times did not record history the way we do. Each writer was inspired by the Holy Spirit and wrote his book for a specific reason and in his own style. Jesus fulfills the history writings in His life.

THE GOSPEL STORY IN THE HISTORY WRITINGS

God's people disobeyed, said they were sorry, obeyed, and disobeyed again, repeating the cycle. They faced consequences for their sin that were severe, including being divided into two different kingdoms, conquered by other nations, and taken into exile, away from the land God had promised them. Even though God's people didn't keep their end of His covenant, God promised He would send His Son to be the good King Israel *really* needed to save them from their sin pattern.

God's people could not obey God on their own. Their hearts loved too many other things, so God sent His Son so that His people could have a new heart, capable of loving God. If you trust Jesus today, you have been given a new heart that doesn't have to be caught in a pattern of disobedience and obedience. You have a heart that can know, love, and serve God joyfully.

MAIN POINTS OF THE HISTORY WRITINGS

1. God is the true and best leader of His people.

God told His people they did not need a king like the other nations because *He* was their King, but they were not satisfied with Him. God gave them the kings they deserved, which led to their disobedience and the consequences of losing their land and being exiled.

2. God cares how we live.

God's people faced consequences because they were not living the good, holy life God instructed them to live. Sin always comes with consequences.

3. God both exiles and delivers.

God is powerful over every nation in the world. He directed every move and even helped nations far from God conquer His people. He did this so that His people would turn back to Him. God exiled His people to other lands as servants, and He delivered them through His power.

KEY IMAGES

Water

God's people crossed the Jordan River to enter the Promised Land, a sort of "baptizing" of God's people in God's land.

Land

God gave each tribe (people group) a particular part of the Promised Land. The History books spend a lot of time talking about the land and its division.

WHERE WAS THIS HAPPENING & WHAT WAS GOING ON IN THE WORLD?

The History books begin as the Israelites crossed the Jordan and entered the Promised Land, Canaan. The books detail Israel's life in the land, as well as their exile from it after they disobeyed God.

Powerful nations that worshiped idols were growing all around God's people. This made God's people want to worship other gods too. The Israelites also did not want to be seen as weak or easy to conquer because they didn't have a king other nations could see. (But they had the most powerful King in the world, because God was their King!)

The Israelites demanded an earthly leader. The History books describe the rise and fall of many kings, as well as the division of the land of Israel into two kingdoms: Judah and Israel, both of which experienced exile. Judah was taken from its land to Babylon, and Israel was taken from its land to Assyria.

The books of Nehemiah and Ezra occurred after the people had lived many years in exile. In these books, God brought His people home to their land. Many people had been in exile so long, though, that they did not return, but stayed. Esther belonged to a family that stayed in the Babylonian Empire, which had been taken over by the Persian Empire. Esther takes place in the Persian capital city, Susa.

THE TRIBAL ALLOTMENTS OF ISRAEL

THINGS YOU NEED TO KNOW

THE TWELVE TRIBES

When God's people entered the Promised Land, they were assigned land by their families. These families are called the **twelve tribes of Israel**, and they come from Jacob's twelve sons (we learn about them in the book of Genesis). Two of Jacob's sons, Levi and Joseph, are not technically included in the twelve tribes who received land. Levi's family, the Levites, were priests. They served in the tabernacle and later, the temple. That family lived among the other tribes. Joseph is not listed because his two sons are. Their names were Ephraim and Manasseh. The twelve tribes are Reuben, Simeon, Judah, Dan, Naphtali, Gad, Asher, Issachar, Zebulun, Ephraim, Manasseh, and Benjamin.

TWO BOOKS IN ONE

The books divided into a first and second book (Samuel, Kings, and Chronicles) were originally one book. The same is true for Ezra and Nehemiah. They tell the story of God's people returning to their land.

A DIVIDED KINGDOM

Israel's first king was Saul, followed by David and then Solomon. Solomon was not as good of a king as his father David. He forced people to build the temple, his fancy palace, and many government buildings. When Solomon's son Rehoboam became king, Rehoboam said he wanted to be even meaner than Solomon. He took the people's money for himself and made it hard for them to survive. A man named Jeroboam complained to Rehoboam, but Rehoboam didn't change. The northern tribes decided Jeroboam would be their king and divided from the southern kingdom.

The northern kingdom was called **Israel**, and the southern kingdom was called **Judah**. These kingdoms had different kings and different capitals. Both kingdoms were exiled for their disobedience to God.

THE IMPORTANCE OF THE TEMPLE

The temple is central in the History writings. It was built in Jerusalem by Solomon and destroyed by King Nebuchadnezzar and his armies a little more than 400 years after it was built. The temple was the location of God's presence and the place of worship for God's people. Its destruction was a picture of Israel's disobedience and broken relationship with God.

THE PROPHETS

The prophets lived and wrote their books of the Bible during the same time as the History writings.

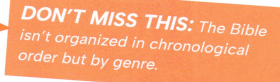

DON'T MISS THIS: The Bible isn't organized in chronological order but by genre.

LOTS OF KINGS

There were *lots* of kings, in both Israel and Judah. Some were faithful and obedient to God, but most were disobedient. Those who are in **blue** were pretty good kings. They pointed people to God. Those in orange were bad kings. They led people away from God. Those who are both colors did some good and some bad.

Saul
David
Solomon
Rehoboam (who caused the division)

JUDAH	ISRAEL
Rehoboam	Jeroboam
Abijah	Nadab
Asa	Baasha
Jehoshaphat	Elah
Jehoram	Zimri
Ahaziah	Omri
Athaliah	Ahab
Joash	Ahaziah
Amaziah	Joram
Uzziah	Jehu
Jotham	Jehoahaz
Ahaz	Jehoash
Hezekiah	Jeroboam II
Manasseh	Zechariah
Amon	Shallum
Josiah	Menahem
Jehoahaz	Pekahiah
Jehoiakim	Pekah
Jehoiachin	Hoshea
Zedekiah	ASSYRIAN CAPTIVITY
BABYLONIAN CAPTIVITY	—722 BC
—586 BC	

KEY QUESTIONS TO ASK & ANSWER WHEN READING THE HISTORY WRITINGS

1. What is true of God, who led the Israelites to the Promised Land and cared for them there?
2. Does this story describe people being faithful or unfaithful to God?
3. What truth in these passages might God want His people to share with others?

PRACTICE IN THE HISTORY WRITINGS

JOSHUA
45. Joshua 1:1–15
46. Joshua 2:1–21
47. Joshua 3:1–17
48. Joshua 5:13–15
49. Joshua 6:1–27
50. Joshua 10:7–15
51. Joshua 20:1–9
52. Joshua 24:1–33

JUDGES
53. Judges 2:1–19
54. Judges 3:12–29
55. Judges 4:1–24
56. Judges 6:11–40
57. Judges 10:6–18
58. Judges 16:1–31

RUTH
59. Ruth 1:8–17
60. Ruth 2:1–17
61. Ruth 2:18–23
62. Ruth 3:1–15
63. Ruth 4:1–22

1 SAMUEL
64. 1 Samuel 1:1–20
65. 1 Samuel 2:1–11
66. 1 Samuel 2:12–36
67. 1 Samuel 3:1–21
68. 1 Samuel 4:1–11
69. 1 Samuel 5:1–12
70. 1 Samuel 6:1–15
71. 1 Samuel 8:1–9, 19–20
72. 1 Samuel 9:1–9, 23–25
73. 1 Samuel 15:10–26
74. 1 Samuel 16:1–13
75. 1 Samuel 17:20–50
76. 1 Samuel 19:1–10
77. 1 Samuel 24:1–22

2 SAMUEL
78. 2 Samuel 5:1–5
79. 2 Samuel 6:1–22
80. 2 Samuel 7:1–17
81. 2 Samuel 11:1–27
82. 2 Samuel 12:1–25
83. 2 Samuel 22:1–51

1 KINGS
84. 1 Kings 3:1–28
85. 1 Kings 6:1–38
86. 1 Kings 8:1–21
87. 1 Kings 9:1–9
88. 1 Kings 11:1–13
89. 1 Kings 12:1–19
90. 1 Kings 17:8–24
91. 1 Kings 18:19–46
92. 1 Kings 19:1–18

2 KINGS
93. 2 Kings 2:1–25
94. 2 Kings 5:1–19
95. 2 Kings 12:1–21
96. 2 Kings 17:1–20
97. 2 Kings 22:1–13; 23:1–3
98. 2 Kings 25:1–21

1 CHRONICLES
99. 1 Chronicles 11:1–19
100. 1 Chronicles 14:8–17; 15:25–29
101. 1 Chronicles 16:1–36
102. 1 Chronicles 17:1–27
103. 1 Chronicles 28:1–21

2 CHRONICLES
104. 2 Chronicles 1:1–17
105. 2 Chronicles 5:1–14
106. 2 Chronicles 7:11–22
107. 2 Chronicles 29:1–36
108. 2 Chronicles 36:15–23

EZRA
109. Ezra 1:1–6
110. Ezra 3:1–13
111. Ezra 6:1–22
112. Ezra 10:1–17

NEHEMIAH
113. Nehemiah 1:1–10
114. Nehemiah 2:1–20
115. Nehemiah 4:1–23
116. Nehemiah 8:2–18
117. Nehemiah 9:1–36
118. Nehemiah 12:27–47

ESTHER
119. Esther 2:1–11, 16–18
120. Esther 2:19–23
121. Esther 3:5–15
122. Esther 5:1–14
123. Esther 7:1–10
124. Esther 8:1–9:2

Passage: Joshua 3:1-17

Date: Today

START-TO-STUDY

1. **PRAY**
2. **READ AND REREAD**

SUMMARIZE OR DRAW A PICTURE OF WHAT YOU READ:

God led the Israelites into the Promised Land. The Jordan River parted like the Red Sea so that they could cross.

---

3. ASK AND ANSWER *Review pages 17 & 18 for help with what to ask.*

ASK:
1. Why did the people stay far behind the ark of the covenant?
2. Were they scared?
3. Did God make Abram into a great nation?
4. Why did the priests need to stand in the water?
5. What does "dispossess" mean?
6. What was the ark of the covenant?
7. How many people crossed the Jordan?
8. Did the Canaanites see them cross?

ANSWER:
1. They knew it was where God dwelled.
2. Probably, but God promised to be with them.
3. Yes.
4. I don't know.
5. God would make the other people leave.
6. The place God dwelled. It was kept in the tabernacle.
7. More than 1,000,000 (Numbers 26).
8. I don't know, but I'm sure word got around fast that new people had come in.

---

4. RESPOND AND PRAY *Write a prayer thanking God for what you learned about Him. Ask God to help you worship Him.*

God, thank You for keeping Your promises to Your people. I love You. In Jesus's name, amen.

Passage: Joshua 3:1-17

START-TO-STUDY
GO DEEPER

Date: Today

GENRE: History

KEY QUESTIONS TO ASK AND ANSWER FOR THIS GENRE:

ASK:
1. What is true of God, who led the Israelites to the Promised Land and cared for them there?
2. Does this story describe people being faithful or unfaithful to God?
3. What truth in this passage might God want His people to share with others?

ANSWER:
1. God is powerful over the waters and kind in the way He lead His people.
2. God's people are being faithful to go into the land.
3. God did what He said He would do! He is always faithful to His promises.

MAIN IDEA: God keeps His promises.

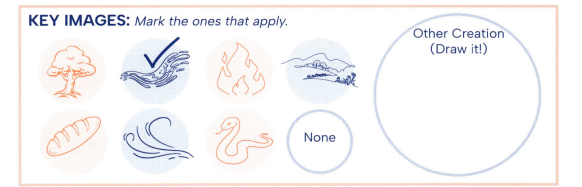

MEMORIZE: Joshua 3:17: The priests carrying the ark of the LORD's covenant stood firmly on dry ground in the middle of the Jordan, while all Israel crossed on dry ground until the entire nation had finished crossing the Jordan.

ALL ABOUT THE HISTORY WRITINGS

JOSHUA

After Moses's death, God called Joshua to lead His people into the Promised Land, where God would give them everything they needed (Joshua 1:3). This was the land God promised would flow with "milk and honey" (Exodus 3:8; Numbers 14:8), meaning the soil was valuable and the farmland was rich in nutrients. God would provide for His people through this great land.

As God's people entered the Promised Land, they faced conflict with the people who lived there: the Canaanites. But God fought for them and gave them victory. Joshua told each tribe where they would live. They began to settle in the land, and they obeyed God—for a while.

The book of Joshua shows how God fulfilled His promise to give His people the Promised Land. Joshua's name means "Yahweh saves." (Yahweh is the Hebrew name of God.) Like Joshua, Jesus would bring His people into a "Promised Land," but a far better one. Those who believe in Jesus will live forever with God in the new heavens and new earth.

See the introduction to the History writings for more about the twelve tribes.

WHO?	Likely Joshua
WHEN?	Around the 15th or 14th century BC
WHERE?	Canaan, the Promised Land
SUBGENRES	Narrative and laws
VERSES TO MEMORIZE	Joshua 1:8–9; 24:15

JUDGES

Judges is filled with more sad stories than any other book of the Bible. God told His people to remove the Canaanites from the land so that the Israelites would not become like them. The people didn't fully obey God, and, after Joshua's death, they became more and more wicked, like the Canaanites.

God appointed judges to rule the people, but even they were disobedient to God's instructions. Judges 21:25 summarizes the book: "In those days there was no king in Israel; everyone did whatever seemed right to him." Not only was there no king, but the people also didn't see God as their King. They did not keep the covenant with Him, and because of their disobedience, God allowed them to lose many battles against their enemies.

Israel had judges who led them to repent and follow God again and judges who led them to disobey God. There were twelve judges: Othniel, Ehud, Shamgar, Deborah, Gideon, Tola, Jair, Jephthah, Ibzan, Elon, Abdon, and Samson. They were not always just or right. Their lives point to a judgment day that is to come, where Jesus will sit on the throne as Judge. He will perfectly and rightly judge all things.

WHO?	Likely Samuel
WHEN?	Spanning from the 14th to the 11th centuries BC
WHERE?	Canaan, the Promised Land
SUBGENRES	Narrative, poetry, and more
VERSE TO MEMORIZE	Judges 21:25

RUTH

Rather than telling the story of all of Israel, the book of Ruth zooms in on one family: Naomi's. A famine in the land caused Naomi's family to move to Moab, a place outside of the Promised Land. Naomi's sons married two women: Ruth and Orpah. Both of the sons and Naomi's husband died. Ruth could have returned to her family, but she decided to stay with Naomi. Ruth became a follower of the one true God, like Naomi.

They returned to the land of Judah together. At this time in history, it was nearly impossible for single women to provide for themselves. Ruth was collecting grain when Boaz, who owned the grain field, noticed her and had compassion on her. He married her and promised to care for her.

God provided for Naomi and Ruth through Boaz, their family redeemer, meaning he was a family member who paid all their debt. Ruth was the grandmother of King David. She is named as a family member of Jesus, our ultimate Redeemer.

WHO?	Likely Samuel
WHEN?	Most likely 1140 BC
WHERE?	Moab and Bethlehem (modern-day Jordan and Israel)
SUBGENRES	Narrative and poetry
VERSE TO MEMORIZE	Ruth 1:16–17

1 SAMUEL

God's people considered 1 and 2 Samuel one book. It tells the story of Israel's first kings and the judge, prophet, and priest who appointed them: Samuel. Even as a small boy, Samuel prophesied about God's coming judgment.

Samuel was right. Some of Israel's enemies, the Philistines, conquered God's people. They took the ark of the covenant, but God punished the Philistines. Eventually, they sent the ark back to Israel.

The Israelites begged for a king, saying they wanted a man named Saul. Saul became king, but he did not obey God. God told Samuel to anoint the next king: a young shepherd boy named David.

Saul knew David would be the next king. He was so jealous, he planned to kill David. David's friend, and Saul's son, Jonathan warned David of Saul's evil plan.

Eventually, David was anointed as king. God called him a "man after his own heart" (1 Samuel 13:14). David was a good king, but one day, the Messiah would come from David's family. He would be the *perfect* King.

WHO?	Likely Samuel (with Gad and Nathan, two other prophets)
WHEN?	11th century BC
WHERE?	In Canaan, the Promised Land
SUBGENRES	Narrative, poetry, prophecy, and more
VERSE TO MEMORIZE	1 Samuel 15:22

2 SAMUEL

Second Samuel continues the story of Israel's first kings. This book begins with the death of Saul. A long war went on between Saul's and David's families, but David was a wise military leader. He brought all the people together under his leadership as king.

God made a **covenant** with David and promised to make his name great. David wanted to build a house for God, but God told David that David's son would do that. This house would be called the **temple**. The most important thing God told David was that He would raise up a King after him who would sit on the throne forever (2 Samuel 7:12–16).

David had many amazing victories, and he tried to honor God, but he was still a sinner. Once, he took a man's wife, Bathsheba, and mistreated her. She became pregnant with David's child. David then sent the man, Uriah, into war so that he would be killed and no one would know what David had done. God sent Nathan, a prophet, to show David his great sin, and David repented. God continued to be with His people, and, while David was a pretty good king, he was not the forever King. That King was coming. God would keep His promise to send a King who would rule forever. His name is Jesus.

WHO?	Likely Samuel (with Gad and Nathan, two other prophets)
WHEN?	Around 1010 BC
WHERE?	In Canaan, the Promised Land
SUBGENRES	Narrative, poetry, and prophecy
VERSE TO MEMORIZE	2 Samuel 22:31

1 KINGS

First and 2 Kings continues the story of Israel's kings, beginning with the death of David and the rise of his son Solomon to the throne—after a bit of competition from another man who wanted to be king. Solomon was a good king at first. He asked God to make him wise and to help him build God's temple. But Solomon saw how he could command people to build beautiful things, and he spent thirteen years building *his* palace. He became the wealthiest man in the world and had many wives, who worshiped other gods. He began to worship those gods too.

When Solomon died, his son Rehoboam took over. He was worse than Solomon and taxed the people mercilessly. The kingdom divided in two: Judah and Israel.

King after king of these two kingdoms was evil. One of these kings was Ahab, whose wife Jezebel tried to get people in Israel to worship the false god Baal. Elijah, a prophet of the one true God, challenged Jezebel's prophets to see whose god was more powerful, his or hers. God showed He was the powerful, true God of all.

This time in history reminded God's people the only truly good King (Jesus) had not come yet.

WHO?	Likely Jeremiah
WHEN?	After David's death, around 970 BC
WHERE?	Judah and Israel
SUBGENRES	Narrative, poetry, prophecy, and more
VERSE TO MEMORIZE	1 Kings 8:23

2 KINGS

God's people divided into two kingdoms: Israel in the north and Judah in the south. Elijah's ministry as a prophet was ending. He had spent years telling the people to repent of their sin and worship God again. But Elijah didn't die. God took him to heaven in a whirlwind rather than allowing him to die on earth.

After Elijah was taken, the prophet Elisha continued telling God's people to repent. God showed His power through Elisha, who performed miracles such as raising a child from the dead and making poisonous water safe. Still, God's people did not turn back to God.

Like 1 Kings, this book records the kings and their spiritual successes and failures. Eventually, both Israel and Judah were conquered. The people were taken from their homes to new lands.

God gave His people many chances to repent and love and follow Him again, but they continued to disobey. Sin matters so much that God came to take care of it Himself. He sent His Son to be a human, live a sinless life, and die on the cross.

WHO?	Likely Jeremiah
WHEN?	After the kingdom divided and until both kingdoms were exiled between 587 and 586 BC
WHERE?	Judah and Israel
SUBGENRES	Narrative and prophecy
VERSE TO MEMORIZE	2 Kings 17:13

1 CHRONICLES

The books of 1 and 2 Chronicles repeat many of the stories found in 1 and 2 Samuel and 1 and 2 Kings, but they were written later, by the priests after they returned to Jerusalem. They wrote the books to record what they wanted God's people to remember from that time in their history.

The first nine chapters in 1 Chronicles are lists of the tribes of Israel. They record who was exiled. The tenth chapter is about Saul's death. The rest of 1 Chronicles focuses on David as king and his plan for the temple. David did not get to build the temple because he sinned against God, Bathsheba, and Uriah, but he did help develop the plans so that Solomon could build it.

This book reminded God's people that God had not forgotten them. Those taken into exile were brought back to the Promised Land. While they missed David as king, they knew they were awaiting a perfect and eternal King.

WHO?	"The Chronicler," likely Ezra
WHEN?	Written after the people returned from exile between 450 and 425 BC
WHERE?	The Promised Land, Canaan
SUBGENRES	Census and narrative
VERSE TO MEMORIZE	1 Chronicles 16:10–11

2 CHRONICLES

Second Chronicles focuses on the four hundred years after King David's reign, which was filled with lots of kings. It repeats much of what is in 2 Kings, but it is recorded from the priest's point of view, after the people returned from exile. It focused on what the priests hoped Israel would remember about the time before they were exiled. It details the temple Solomon built in Jerusalem and the worship that occurred there.

The kings who reigned after Solomon were almost all evil, with very few exceptions. God's people worshiped idols and disobeyed Him, and He brought judgment against them through Assyria and Babylon. These two nations conquered and exiled both Israel and Judah as a consequence of their great sin.

We may face consequences for sin on earth, but we do not have to worry about being spiritually exiled—or separated from God—because of Jesus. He has made us right with God through His death on the cross.

DON'T MISS THIS: The priests were writing at a time when the temple was in ruins. No worship could occur.

WHO?	"The Chronicler," likely Ezra
WHEN?	Written after the people returned from exile between 450 and 425 BC
WHERE?	The Promised Land, Canaan
SUBGENRES	Narrative and poetry
VERSE TO MEMORIZE	2 Chronicles 7:14

EZRA

Ezra and Nehemiah are one book in the Hebrew Bible. Together, they tell the story of God's people returning to Israel after being in Babylonian captivity. Ezra records the return of two different groups of Israelites. The first group was led by a religious leader named Zerubbabel (Ezra 1–6). The second group returned about sixty years later. They were led by Ezra.

The kings around Jerusalem did not want Israel to be strong again, so they tried to stop the people from rebuilding the temple and the city's walls. Ezra records many letters between key leaders talking about this.

God provided for His people with King Darius. This king had compassion on Israel and paid for the rebuilding. He also told the other leaders to leave them alone.

God's people mourned because the second temple wasn't as glorious as the first, but they still praised and worshiped God, and Ezra read from the scroll (the Law). The rebuilding of the second temple was a picture of what was to come: God fully restoring His people to Himself through His Son, Jesus.

WHO?	Likely Ezra
WHEN?	Written around 400 BC
WHERE?	In Israel's capital, Jerusalem
SUBGENRES	Narrative, poetry, letters, and census
VERSE TO MEMORIZE	Ezra 3:11

NEHEMIAH

The book of Nehemiah finishes the story started by Ezra. It tells about the return of the exiled people to Jerusalem so that they could rebuild the temple and the walls of the city.

Nehemiah was an important leader in King Artaxerxes's palace. He was the cupbearer, which meant he was a trusted person who would taste the king's food and drinks before he ate or drank them to make sure they were not poisoned. Even with this important role, the king let Nehemiah go to Jerusalem to help rebuild his home. Leaders still tried to keep God's people from finishing the walls, but God's people did not stop working on them.

Nehemiah is the last book before the New Testament chronologically. Esther, which comes after Nehemiah, happened during the time recorded by Ezra. The prophet Malachi prophesied while Nehemiah was rebuilding the walls. God's people were back in their Promised Land; now, they were waiting for their promised King.

WHO?	Likely Nehemiah
WHEN?	Written around 400 BC
WHERE?	Persia and Jerusalem
SUBGENRES	Narrative and poetry
VERSE TO MEMORIZE	Nehemiah 8:10

ESTHER

Esther was a Jew who had been exiled to Susa in Persia. Her cousin, Mordecai, looked after her there.

After Vashti, queen of Persia, made King Xerxes angry, he ran a contest to pick the next queen. Esther was very beautiful, and the king loved her more than any other. He didn't know she was one of God's people. One day when Mordecai was near the palace checking on Esther, he overheard a plot to kill the king. He told Esther and she told the king. They saved the king!

Later, Haman, an evil leader in Susa, came up with a plan to kill all the Jews. He got the king to sign a law that would let people hurt the Jews. Esther threw a banquet so that she could tell the king about Haman's plan. When the king understood the law he had signed, he sent Haman to be killed. Then, he gave Mordecai the ability to help create laws in the land. Mordecai had saved the king earlier, and now the king was saving Mordecai, Esther, and all God's people.

God is not directly mentioned in Esther, but He was obviously at work, protecting His people. Esther intervened with King Xerxes to save her people. In an even bigger way, Jesus intervenes on behalf of God's children so that they will be saved.

WHO?	Unknown (Jewish tradition says it was "The Men of the Great Assembly", which still doesn't tell us much)
WHEN?	Likely between 486 and 465 BC (in the time between Ezra 6 and 7)
WHERE?	Susa, Persia
SUBGENRES	Narrative, poetry, and more
VERSES TO MEMORIZE	Esther 4:14

GENRE: WISDOM

THE WISDOM WRITINGS highlight what wisdom is and how to find it through story, poetry, wise sayings, and teachings. They include:

- **Job**
- **Psalms**
- **Proverbs**
- **Ecclesiastes**
- **Song of Songs**

Each book is quite different, making this category of biblical writing interesting and fun to read!

What is wisdom? Wisdom is the knowledge of what is good and right and using that knowledge to make decisions. Jesus is Wisdom.

Wisdom writings were a popular genre in the ancient Near East. The wisest sages, or leaders with lots of wisdom and knowledge, taught people the wise path to the good life. They told people, who told others, who told more. This is called being passed down **orally**.

The books in this section of the Bible range from the time of Moses to the time of David and Solomon. They address the most difficult questions we face in our lives like, *Why do bad things happen?* and *Why does life feel like it doesn't have a purpose sometimes?*

They also touch on every emotion we might experience: sadness, fear, frustration, happiness, excitement, confusion, anger, hopelessness, hope, amazement, happiness, gratefulness, contentment, love, and more. **These books show us that God is not made smaller by our questions or our feelings.** He welcomes us to talk to Him about it all.

The Wisdom writings teach us the wise way to live: obeying God's laws with our whole selves. God has always been after our complete worship: *knowing* Him with our heads, *loving* Him with our hearts, and *serving* Him with our hands. We worship Him with our whole selves—including our questions and our emotions—all so that we can praise God and live wisely

> **DON'T MISS THIS:** Jesus is Wisdom. As Christians, to live with wisdom is to live like Jesus.

WHERE ARE WE IN THE STORY?

The Wisdom writings are part of the storylines in the Law and History writings. They were written throughout the introduction to God and His people and in times of crisis by people like Moses, David, and Solomon.

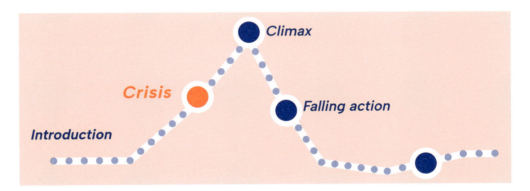

HOW TO READ WISDOM WRITINGS

Each wisdom book is different from the others. **Job** is a story that must be read as a whole. But you can read a chapter or even a verse of the **Psalms** and **Proverbs** to understand it on its own. **Ecclesiastes** is intentionally long and repetitive to point out the truth that without God, life is long and repetitive and without purpose. **Song of Songs** is a long poem about a husband's great love for his wife, but it has a double meaning—it also shows God's love for His people. Each book is an adventure all its own!

THE GOSPEL STORY IN THE WISDOM WRITINGS

The Wisdom writings show us what Jesus is like because He is wisdom. To live a wise life is to love and follow Jesus. We can't be truly wise on our own, but when we trust Jesus, we are made new and given the mind of Christ (1 Corinthians 2:16). And with the Holy Spirit, whom Jesus sent to help His people after He left earth, we can choose wisdom rather than foolishness.

MAIN POINTS OF THE WISDOM WRITINGS

1. Wise people fear the Lord.

God has not left us to figure out how to live wisely on our own. Instead, He told us how to be wise: by knowing and loving Him with our hearts, souls, minds, and strength.

2. God's wisdom is better than riches.

God asks us to *seek* wisdom (Jesus), which means to run hard after it. It is better to be wise than to be the richest person in the world. Solomon was the richest man ever, yet Ecclesiastes says riches don't bring anyone—including Solomon—purpose or happiness. We can only have a good, wise life by following God.

3. Worship is a team sport.

In the books of Wisdom, God makes it clear that people need one another to live the good life He has designed. The purpose of some wisdom books, specifically Psalms, was to provide songs and praises that God's people could sing to Him *together*.

KEY IMAGES

Trees

The Psalms describe the wise person as a tree planted by streams of water, meaning, they're being nourished by God's Spirit and are growing strong in obedience to God.

Water

Wells are mentioned often in the Wisdom writings. Psalms even says that God has turned dead and empty wildernesses into oases of water (Psalm 107:35–36). Water is a picture of God's ability to bring life to dead places, because water is a source of life.

WHERE WAS THIS HAPPENING & WHAT WAS GOING ON IN THE WORLD?

Like the other books in the Old Testament, these books were written in the ancient Near East, from modern-day Egypt to modern-day Israel, and lots of places in between. God's people constantly went from disobeying God to obeying Him, from wise living to living in rebellion against God. The people who wrote these words—from Moses and David to Solomon and other writers—were inspired by God the Holy Spirit. They were real people dealing with many things we deal with today.

THINGS YOU NEED TO KNOW

CHIASM

Chiasms are types of poems. They place words or concepts in a particular order and then repeat them in reverse. They are used in every book of the Wisdom writings. Psalm 1 is a great example of a chiasm. The most important point of a chiasm is found in the middle.

COMPARE & CONTRAST

Many books of Wisdom lean on comparisons and contrasts to highlight the point God is making. In Proverbs 10, Solomon uses these elements to highlight the difference between the righteous person and the wicked person. Proverbs 10:16–17 says,

> *The reward of the righteous is life;*
> *the wages of the wicked is punishment.*
>
> *The one who follows instruction is on the path to life,*
> *but the one who rejects correction goes astray.*

The righteous listens to and obeys God's instruction, which leads to life. The wicked does not listen to nor obey God's instruction, and this leads to punishment. A person could be one or the other: righteous or wicked. But he or she could not be both.

FIGURATIVE LANGUAGE

In poetry, the writer may exaggerate to make a point. This is called **hyperbole**, and Psalm 42:3 is an example: "My tears have been my food day and night, while all day long people say to me, 'Where is your God?'" The writer hasn't really been eating his tears. He means he is so upset that he has not eaten all day. He has only cried.

Ecclesiastes uses hyperbole when it says that *all things are meaningless*. Obviously, we can find meaning and enjoyment in things, but the author of Ecclesiastes is showing that true meaning is only found in God.

Personification is a type of writing that gives person-like characteristics to things that aren't people. Psalm 98:8 says, "Let the rivers clap their hands, let the mountains sing together for joy." This psalm uses rivers that don't have hands and mountains that can't sing to say that all the earth will praise God.

Similes compare two things using the words "like" or "as." **Metaphors** compare two things that are not similar without using the words "like" or "as."

Psalm 119:105 includes a metaphor: "Your word is a lamp for my feet and a light on my path." The Bible is not *literally* a lamp that can be turned on so our feet don't trip over things in the floor. But it does help us make wise choices about our "next steps" in our journeys with God.

Song of Songs 4:1–3 includes multiple similes. The author compares his beloved's hair to "a flock of goats streaming down Mount Gilead," her teeth to "a flock of newly shorn sheep coming up from washing, each one bearing twins, and none has lost its young," her lips to "a scarlet cord," and her brow to "a slice of pomegranate."

The big metaphor of Ecclesiastes compares the meaninglessness of life to chasing after the wind. No one can chase the wind, but the phrase shows it's frustrating to search for something you can't find. No one can find purpose and value anywhere besides God.

KEY QUESTIONS TO ASK & ANSWER WHEN READING WISDOM WRITINGS

1. How does this passage praise God, who gives wisdom?
2. How does this passage help me know and love Jesus?
3. How are wisdom and foolishness being compared?
4. How can I live as a wise person who follows Jesus?

PRACTICE IN THE WISDOM WRITINGS

JOB
125. Job 1:1–22
126. Job 2:1–13
127. Job 25:1–26:14
128. Job 28:1–28
129. Job 32:1–22
130. Job 37:1–24
131. Job 38:1–42
132. Job 42:1–17

PSALMS
133. Psalm 1
134. Psalm 23
135. Psalm 30
136. Psalm 37
137. Psalm 40
138. Psalm 46
139. Psalm 51
140. Psalm 62
141. Psalm 84
142. Psalm 91
143. Psalm 103
144. Psalm 106
145. Psalm 119
146. Psalm 121
147. Psalm 139

PROVERBS
148. Proverbs 1
149. Proverbs 2
150. Proverbs 3
151. Proverbs 4
152. Proverbs 9
153. Proverbs 10
154. Proverbs 15
155. Proverbs 21
156. Proverbs 27
157. Proverbs 31

ECCLESIASTES
158. Ecclesiastes 1:1–18
159. Ecclesiastes 3:1–22
160. Ecclesiastes 9:1–18
161. Ecclesiastes 12:1–14

SONG OF SONGS
162. Song of Songs 1:1–11
163. Song of Songs 3:1–11
164. Song of Songs 6:1–12

Passage: Psalm 1

START-TO-STUDY

Date: Today

1. PRAY
2. READ AND REREAD

SUMMARIZE OR DRAW A PICTURE OF WHAT YOU READ:

Psalm 1 contrasts the righteous and the wicked.

3. ASK AND ANSWER *Review pages 17 & 18 for help with what to ask.*

ASK:
1. Is this poetry?
2. Is there any figurative writing?
3. How do I meditate on God's Word?
4. What does it mean to wither?
5. What does it mean to prosper?
6. What is chaff?
7. What does it mean that the wicked won't stand in judgment?
8. Why would righteousness bring happiness or delight?
9. Why does it seem like the wicked succeed sometimes?
10. How do we know God watches over the righteous?

ANSWER:
1. Yes.
2. There are metaphors: the righteous are like a tree planted by water; the wicked are like chaff.
3. Read and reread it. Focus on it.
4. This is when leaves are dying.
5. Success or good things happen.
6. The useless part of wheat.
7. I need to ask my mom. I don't know.
8. God's way is best.
9. The wicked might succeed for a while but not forever.
10. We may not feel Him watching, but God sees everything and is in control of it all. God cares for His people.

4. RESPOND AND PRAY *Write a prayer thanking God for what you learned about Him. Ask God to help you worship Him.*

God, thank You for watching over the way of the righteous. Help me follow You. Thank You for Jesus, who came so that I could be called righteous, not because of anything I can do but because of what Jesus did for me. In Jesus's name, amen.

Passage: Psalm 11:1-2

START-TO-STUDY
GO DEEPER

Date: Today

GENRE: Wisdom / poetry

KEY QUESTIONS TO ASK AND ANSWER FOR THIS GENRE:

ASK:
1. How does this passage praise the God, who gives wisdom?
2. How does this passage help me know and love Jesus?
3. How are wisdom and foolishness being compared?
4. How can I live as a wise person who follows Jesus?

ANSWER:
1. It tells me God watches over the righteous and helps them.
2. The wise don't walk in the advice of the wicked or stand in the pathway with sinners or sit in the company of mockers. They delight in God's instruction. Jesus taught us about God because He is God.
3. The wise obey God and are like a healthy tree. The wicked are like chaff. They cannot stand up in judgment.
4. I can ask God to help me love His Word, like Jesus did, and obey God.

MAIN IDEA: The righteous will succeed, but the wicked will not.

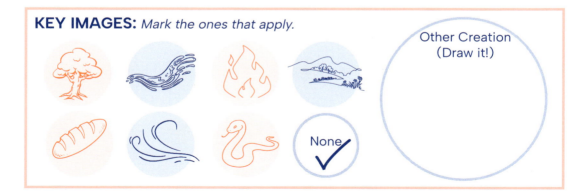

KEY IMAGES: *Mark the ones that apply.*

Other Creation (Draw it!)

None ✓

MEMORIZE: Psalm 11:1-2: I have taken refuge in the Lord. How can you say to me, "Escape to the mountains like a bird! For look, the wicked string bows; they put their arrows on bowstrings to shoot from the shadows at the upright in heart."

ALL ABOUT THE WISDOM WRITINGS

JOB

The book of Job is a series of conversations between God and Satan, Job and his friends, and Job and God. God lets Satan bring hard times to Job because Satan thought the hard times would make Job turn away from God. Job faced every kind of tragedy, but he did not blame God or turn away from Him. Job's friends quietly sit with him for a couple of weeks, comforting him, before they try to explain why these bad things must have happened to Job.

Throughout the book, it's important to notice who is talking in each section. Job's friends ask him to confess his sin and repent. They think he must have done something to cause his suffering, but neither of his friends nor Job knew that Satan brought all of the hard, sad things to Job. None of it was Job's fault. God speaks His wisdom through a whirlwind, answering Job's questions and reminding Job that He is powerful and good, even when suffering comes. Hard times come for us all, no matter how closely we follow God. There's only been one who was perfect—Jesus. He faced *suffering for* us so that our sins can be forgiven.

WHO?	Unknown
WHEN?	We don't know, but it could be around the time Abraham, Isaac, or Jacob lived
WHERE?	Uz, which is probably near modern-day Jordan
SUBGENRES	Narrative and poetry
VERSES TO MEMORIZE	Job 23:12; 42:2

PSALMS

Psalm 1 summarizes the book: Wisdom is found in being like a tree planted by streams of water, or being firm in following God and His Word. The Psalms give us an example of how to pray and remind us that God welcomes our raw emotions. There are different kinds of psalms within the book: praise (worship), lament (poems of sadness), thanksgiving (gratefulness to God), royal (worshiping God as King), and hymns (songs written to be sung with music).

The Psalms are divided into five books.
- Book 1: Psalms 1–41
- Book 2: Psalms 42–72
- Book 3: Psalms 73–89
- Book 4: Psalms 90–106
- Book 5: Psalms 107–150

The Psalms teach deep truths about God, as well as His willingness to be with us in our suffering. Jesus understands suffering because He has felt it. There's nothing in our lives that God is not willing to walk through with us.

WHO?	David, Asaph, Korah and his sons, Moses, Solomon, Ethan, Heman, and unnamed authors
WHEN?	From the time of Moses to Solomon, spanning about 1,000 years from the 15th century BC to the 6th century or later
WHERE?	From the wilderness where the Israelites wandered to the Promised Land
SUBGENRES	Poetry
VERSES TO MEMORIZE	Psalms 1:1–2; 27:4; 56:3; 139:13–14

PROVERBS

Proverbs is focused on helping people know how to live a wise life, which is a life lived for God. It is one of the most unique books in the Bible. It includes some longer wisdom writing that might be a chapter or more, but most of the proverbs are short sayings that were (and are) easy to memorize.

When you read Proverbs, it's important to remember these are wise pieces of *advice*, not *promises* that will be kept in our lives perfectly. Sometimes, you may live for God just as He's asked, and bad things still happen because sin is in the world. However, we can trust that God will fulfill the wisdom in Proverbs through Jesus in eternity.

God is the giver of wisdom, and we see God's wisdom in His Son, Jesus. Jesus shows us how to live a perfectly wise life—by trusting in and following Him.

WHO?	Solomon, Agur, and Lemuel
WHEN?	During Solomon's life, probably in the 900s BC
WHERE?	The Promised Land, Canaan
SUBGENRES	Poetry
VERSES TO MEMORIZE	Proverbs 3:5–6; 16:24

ECCLESIASTES

Ecclesiastes is a long, repetitive book that reminds the reader that everything in life is pointless if someone's life isn't lived for God. No amount of money or important work or enjoyment will make anyone happy for their whole life. The author repeats phrases like "all is vanity under the sun" to remind the reader that life feels repetitive and pointless without God.

Even for Christians, frustrations and difficult seasons are unavoidable. But we are never without hope. Ecclesiastes 3:11 says God has written eternity on our hearts. We are made for more than this world can offer, so we will always long for heaven. Jesus is the answer to the "vanities" of Ecclesiastes. If we are following Him, nothing is meaningless.

WHO?	"The Teacher," who many believe was Solomon
WHEN?	Sometime around 935 BC
WHERE?	The Promised Land, Canaan
SUBGENRES	Poetry and sermons
VERSE TO MEMORIZE	Ecclesiastes 3:11

SONG OF SONGS

Song of Songs (also known as Song of Solomon) is the last of the Wisdom books. The title comes from the first verse of the book, and it means the writer thought this was the *best* song of *all* the songs.

It is a long poem that records the conversation of a man and a woman who love one another and their friends who support them. It can also be described as a love song between husband and wife. It's unclear if this book is about a real relationship between the writer and a woman, or if it is a poem that teaches about love but is not about real people. Song of Songs has lots of repetition, similes, and metaphors. It is the only book that is one long poem.

God created men and women in His image. This book is a poetic love story that points back to the good relationships in the garden of Eden, before sin entered the world. God created marriage as the best place for a physical relationship between a man and a woman. Husbands and wives are to love one another and stay loyal to one another, because this is how God created marriage. Marriage is a metaphor for the love between Jesus and the church. God wants marriages to show His love.

WHO?	Probably Solomon
WHEN?	Sometime during Solomon's reign
WHERE?	The Promised Land, Canaan
SUBGENRES	Poetry
VERSES TO MEMORIZE	Song of Songs 1:4

THE PROPHETS

GENRE: THE PROPHETS

THE PROPHETS include seventeen books:

1. Isaiah
2. Jeremiah
3. Lamentations
4. Ezekiel
5. Daniel
6. Hosea
7. Joel
8. Amos
9. Obadiah
10. Jonah
11. Micah
12. Nahum
13. Habakkuk
14. Zephaniah
15. Haggai
16. Zechariah
17. Malachi

The Prophets get their name from the people who wrote this genre of the Bible: God's prophets. For clarity, when the word *Prophet* is capitalized, it's referring to the genre. When the word *prophet* is lowercase, it refers to the type of person.

A prophet was a messenger who took the words they received from God and communicated them to God's people. These messages were difficult to deliver because they were warnings to the people. If God's people didn't change their way of living and turn back to God, God would condemn them. He would punish their sin to remind them that they needed to follow the one true God. These writers aren't the first prophets mentioned in Scripture—people like Moses, Samuel, Nathan, Elijah, and Elisha also brought messages from God to people.

The books in this genre begin when the kingdom of Israel divides and end after the exile. Many of the things described in the History books are happening while the Prophets are being written. If the books of History are the plot, the Prophets are the dialogue.

The Prophets are not arranged in chronological order. They are organized by their length: Major Prophets are longer books of prophecy, while Minor Prophets are shorter. The five Major Prophets are Isaiah, Jeremiah, Lamentations, Ezekiel, and Daniel. The twelve Minor Prophets are Hosea, Joel, Amos, Obadiah, Jonah, Micah, Nahum, Habakkuk, Zephaniah, Haggai, Zechariah, and Malachi.

DON'T MISS THIS: The Major prophets aren't more important than the Minor Prophets.

When you hear the word *prophecy*, you may think of a prediction about something that will happen in the future. More often, though, the Prophets explain what was happening at that time in history. Sometimes, the message is both. It tells what was happening and foretells what was to come, such as God's judgment or the coming of the Messiah.

WHERE ARE WE IN THE STORY?

Throughout the Prophets, the crisis continues to build. People keep turning away from God and toward sin. But in this genre, God begins to show His people what the answer to their problems will be: a Messiah who will save them from their greatest enemy. The climax hasn't come yet, but it's on its way.

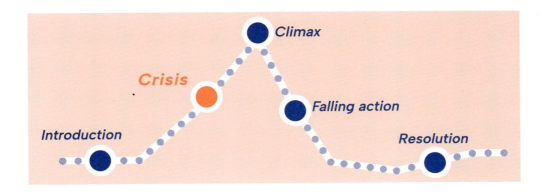

HOW TO READ THE PROPHETS

The Prophets spoke to a particular person or group of people at a particular time, so it can be hard for us to understand them easily. We aren't those people, and we don't live during that time. As you read, pay attention to whom each prophet is talking to. What problem is the prophet discussing? How are the people responding to the prophet and his message? Are they listening? Rejecting? Ignoring?

THE GOSPEL STORY IN THE PROPHETS

The Prophets delivered difficult news to God's people, including God's judgment for their sin and their exile. There were real consequences for the people's sin, and they included the very sad result of being taken from their home—the place where they could worship God.

Still, God promised they wouldn't be exiled forever. The Prophets told the people that God would bring them home one day (Jeremiah 29:14). But even better than God bringing them back to the Promised Land was the promise that God's Son would bring them back to closeness with God in their hearts. God's Son, Jesus, would pay for sin once and for all on the cross so that they (and we) could have a right relationship with God and live forever in His good kingdom.

DON'T MISS THIS: Remember, exile is when God's people were taken from their land by a foreign army and made to live somewhere far from their home. They also had to serve their enemies and were told to worship false gods.

MAIN POINTS OF THE PROPHETS

1. God cares about justice.
God does not ignore the mistreatment of people. He knows about and will take care of injustice in His timing.

2. God gave many opportunities for repentance.
The Prophets warned people of God's judgment. If they repented (or turned away from their sin and worshiped God), they would not experience that judgment. They had many chances to turn back to God.

3. While God promised to bring His people back home, a better homecoming is still on its way.
In the most difficult times, when God's people were rebelling against Him and about to be exiled, Jeremiah delivered a message of hope (Jeremiah 33:31–34). God would begin a new covenant with His people through the Messiah. This covenant would bring forgiveness for sin forever because the Messiah would die to pay for sin. Everyone who trusts in the Messiah—that's Jesus—is brought into the family of God, ultimately being kept forever at home with Him.

What does Messiah mean? Messiah means "anointed one" or "chosen one." Jesus is the Son of God—the only One chosen and anointed to take away the sins of the world!

KEY IMAGES

Trees

The Prophets compare God's people to trees and plants, whether healthy or withering. In Isaiah 41:19, God promises to put healthy trees in the desert—a promise to bring life out of what seems to be a lifeless space.

Marriage

Ezekiel and Hosea both use marriage as an example of the covenant between God and His people.

WHERE WAS THIS HAPPENING & WHAT WAS GOING ON IN THE WORLD?

The prophets were sent by God during the time of the divided kingdom. They continued to prophesy even after God's people had been exiled by Assyria and Babylon, and as they returned to the Promised Land under King Cyrus. This time overlaps with the books of Kings, Chronicles, Ezra, and Nehemiah. The Prophets were written in places all over the modern-day Middle East.

THINGS YOU NEED TO KNOW

EXILE IS A THEME IN THE BIBLE

The Prophets record messages from God in the times before, during, and after His people were exiled. This wasn't the first time God's people were exiled; Adam and Eve were exiled from the garden of Eden. Sin sets us far from God—exiled from Him—but trusting in Jesus brings us home to Him forever.

THE PROMISE OF A NEW COVENANT

Even when God's people disobeyed Him and experienced hard things, God promised to create a new covenant (or promise) with them. This promise is hinted at throughout the Prophets. The new covenant would not replace the old covenant that God gave Moses in Exodus—it would make it complete! God would send someone we call the Messiah, who could perfectly keep God's law of the old covenant and have no sin.

The Messiah extends the **new covenant** to anyone who follows Him. This covenant is not based on the laws in Exodus, Leviticus, or Deuteronomy; it's based on a sinless sacrifice. Jesus is the Messiah, and He paid for our sins on the cross and rose from the dead, victorious over sin. Through Him, we are made right with God and have the Holy Spirit to lead and guide us. Through Jesus, God kept the promises He made through the Prophets.

> **DON'T MISS THIS:** Jeremiah 31:33–34 is an example of a prophecy of the new covenant. God promises He will put His law on His people's minds and hearts, forgive their sins, and allow them to truly know Him.

WHO WERE THEY PROPHESYING TO?

The prophets weren't all talking to the same people. God delivered messages to multiple groups of people through His prophets. Here's who they spoke to:

Sent to Israel	*Sent to Judah*	*Sent to Nineveh*	*Sent to Edom*	*Sent to Judah's exiles in Babylon*	*Sent to exiles who had returned to Judah*
Amos Hosea	Joel Isaiah Micah Zephaniah Jeremiah Habakkuk	Jonah Nahum	Obadiah	Ezekiel Daniel Haggai	Haggai Zechariah Malachi

WHEN DID THE PROPHETS PROPHESY?

Prophet	When? Sometime around:	Bible passages about them:
Jonah	786–746 BC	2 Kings 14:25; Jonah
Hosea	786–746	Hosea
Amos	760–698	Amos
Isaiah	740–698	2 Kings 19–20; Isaiah
Micah	735–710	Jeremiah 26:18; Micah
Nahum	680–612	Nahum
Zephaniah	640–621	Zephaniah
Jeremiah	626–584	2 Chronicles 36:12; Jeremiah
Habakkuk	608–598	Habakkuk
Daniel	605–539*	Ezekiel 14:14; 14:20; 28:3; Ezra 8:2; Daniel
Ezekiel	593–571	Ezekiel
Obadiah	580	Obadiah
Joel	539–331	Joel
Haggai	520	Ezra 5:1; 6:14; Haggai
Zechariah	520–514	Ezra 5:1; 6:14; Zechariah
Malachi	500–450	Malachi

*The dates of Daniel's prophecy have been argued by people for a long time, but we know he was in Babylon during the exile, so these dates are our best guess.

KEY QUESTIONS TO ASK & ANSWER WHEN READING THE PROPHETS

1. What does this passage show me God cares about?
2. What is God's message to the people?
3. Are the people responding rightly to the message?
4. What happens because of the people's response?

PRACTICE IN THE PROPHETS

ISAIAH
165. Isaiah 6:1–13
166. Isaiah 9:1–7
167. Isaiah 11:1–16
168. Isaiah 24:1–23
169. Isaiah 30:18–26
170. Isaiah 35:1–10
171. Isaiah 43:1–28
172. Isaiah 53:1–12
173. Isaiah 61:1–11
174. Isaiah 65:17–25

JEREMIAH
175. Jeremiah 1:1–19
176. Jeremiah 9:1–16
177. Jeremiah 11:1–23
178. Jeremiah 13:1–11
179. Jeremiah 23:1–8
180. Jeremiah 29:4–20
181. Jeremiah 31:31–40
182. Jeremiah 36:16–32
183. Jeremiah 39:1–18
184. Jeremiah 50:17–32

LAMENTATIONS
185. Lamentations 1:1–22
186. Lamentations 3:1–24
187. Lamentations 5:1–22

EZEKIEL
188. Ezekiel 1:1–28
189. Ezekiel 2:1–9
190. Ezekiel 4:1–17
191. Ezekiel 6:1–14
192. Ezekiel 11:1–25
193. Ezekiel 20:1–20
194. Ezekiel 25:1–17
195. Ezekiel 34:1–30
196. Ezekiel 37:1–14
197. Ezekiel 40:1–4; 43:1–12
198. Ezekiel 47:1–12

DANIEL
199. Daniel 1:1–21
200. Daniel 2:1–30
201. Daniel 3:1–30
202. Daniel 5:1–31
203. Daniel 6:1–28
204. Daniel 9:1–19
205. Daniel 10:1–21

HOSEA
206. Hosea 1:1–11
207. Hosea 2:14–23
208. Hosea 6:1–11
209. Hosea 9:1–9
210. Hosea 11:1–12
211. Hosea 14:1–9

JOEL
212. Joel 1:1–15
213. Joel 2:12–32

AMOS
214. Amos 3:1–11
215. Amos 5:1–15
216. Amos 7:1–9
217. Amos 9:1–15

OBADIAH
218. Obadiah 1:1–21

JONAH
219. Jonah 1:1–17
220. Jonah 2:1–10
221. Jonah 3:1–10
222. Jonah 4:1–11

MICAH
223. Micah 2:1–13
224. Micah 3:1–12
225. Micah 7:8–12

NAHUM
226. Nahum 1:1–15

HABAKKUK
227. Habakkuk 1:1–17
228. Habakkuk 3:16–19

ZEPHANIAH
229. Zephaniah 1:1–18
230. Zephaniah 3:9–20

HAGGAI
231. Haggai 1:1–15
232. Haggai 2:1–23

ZECHARIAH
233. Zechariah 1:1–21
234. Zechariah 8:1–23
235. Zechariah 10:1–12
236. Zechariah 14:1–21

MALACHI
237. Malachi 4:1–6

Passage: Isaiah 6:1–13

START-TO-STUDY

Date: Today

1. **PRAY**
2. **READ AND REREAD**

SUMMARIZE OR DRAW A PICTURE OF WHAT YOU READ:

God showed His glory to Isaiah and called him to go and to speak about Him.

3. ASK AND ANSWER *Review pages 17 & 18 for help with what to ask.*

ASK:

1. What are seraphim?
2. Was Isaiah scared?
3. Why did Isaiah say, "Woe is me"?
4. What does holy mean?
5. Why did the seraphim touch Isaiah's mouth with a hot coal?
6. Why is God allowing the cities to "lie in ruins"?
7. Does God still call people like this today?

ANSWER:

1. Creatures around God's throne.
2. Probably.
3. He saw how unholy he was when he compared himself to the holiness of God.
4. Different, separate, perfect, whole.
5. Ouch. His mouth, which would tell the truth about God, was being purified.
6. God's judgment is being poured out because of the people's disobedience.
7. He can!

4. RESPOND AND PRAY *Write a prayer thanking God for what you learned about Him. Ask God to help you worship Him.*

God, thank You for using prophets to show what is true about You. Thank You for being so patient with my disobedience. I love You. In Jesus's name, amen.

Passage: Isaiah 6:1-3

START-TO-STUDY
GO DEEPER

Date: Today

GENRE: Prophecy

KEY QUESTIONS TO ASK AND ANSWER FOR THIS GENRE:

ASK:
1. What does this passage show me God cares about?
2. What is God's message to the people?
3. Are the people responding rightly to the message?
4. What happens because of the people's response?

ANSWER:
1. God cares that His messengers are pure. God sends people who are willing to carry His messengers to others.
2. Isaiah was to tell the people, "Be ever hearing, but never understanding." God was telling them that they do not listen or obey Him.
3. We don't know yet, but it seems like they won't because Isaiah had to tell them this until the cities lie in ruin.
4. Seems like the city was destroyed and God's people were exiled.

MAIN IDEA: God leads us to worship and to tell others His truth by showing us His glory.

KEY IMAGES: Mark the ones that apply.

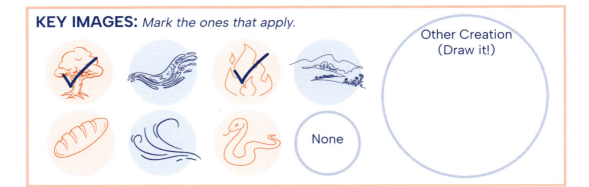

MEMORIZE: Isaiah 6:8: Then I heard the voice of the Lord asking: "Who will I send? Who will go for us?" I said: "Here I am. Send me."

ALL ABOUT THE PROPHETS

ISAIAH
Major Prophet

The prophet Isaiah is sent to the leaders of Israel and Judah to warn them that they would be exiled by other nations if they did not turn back to God. He told them the nation of Israel would be chopped down like a tree (Isaiah 10:34), or totally destroyed. But one day, a sprout would come from that stump of a dead tree and bring new life. As the book continues, Isaiah's prophecy comes true. God's people are exiled and then brought back. Some people repent; others continue to stay far from God.

Isaiah describes a Servant-King who would come, suffer, and die for His people (chapters 50–53). This person would make a way for people to be with God forever. Because Isaiah clearly tells the *good news* still to come, this book is often called the Fifth Gospel.

WHO?	Isaiah (some people believe other writers helped toward the end)
WHEN?	During the reign of Uzziah, Jotham, Ahaz, and Hezekiah, into exile and beyond (between 740 and 698 BC)
WHERE?	In Judah and Israel
SUBGENRES	Poetry, prose, sermons, narrative, and apocalyptic
VERSES TO MEMORIZE	Isaiah 9:6; 53:6

JEREMIAH
Major Prophet

As the son of a priest, Jeremiah knew God's laws and covenants well. God sent him to warn Judah about all the ways they had broken God's covenant. Jeremiah told them the nation of Babylon would exile them if they did not return to God. The people rejected Jeremiah and his message. They threatened him, and they even kidnapped him and took him to Egypt once. Jeremiah is often called the "weeping prophet," because he was saddened by the people's hard hearts and everything they went through, such as exile.

God's people were exiled, and Jeremiah continued to speak to them during this time. He spoke of God's wrath against Babylon. He also promised God would create a new covenant. This covenant would make a way for people to love and obey God because God's law would be written on their hearts.

DON'T MISS THIS: This book is an anthology. That's a big word! An anthology is a collection of writings. This one is from and about Jeremiah and was organized by a scribe (Baruch) who wrote and edited things.

WHO?	Jeremiah (with the help of a scribe named Baruch)
WHEN?	During the reigns of Josiah, Jehoahaz, Jehoiakim, Jehoiachin, and Zedekiah, and into the exile (around 626–584 BC)
WHERE?	Judah and Babylon
SUBGENRES	Narrative, poetry, and apocalyptic
VERSES TO MEMORIZE	Jeremiah 1:7–8; 31:31–34

LAMENTATIONS
Major Prophet

Lamentations is a book of poetry that communicates the pain, suffering, and confusion of God's people when their capital city, Jerusalem, and their place of worship, the temple, were attacked and conquered by the Babylonians. In only five chapters, Lamentations records how God's people felt as the Promised Land was taken. The poems of chapters 1–4 are **acrostics**. Each line begins with a letter from the Hebrew alphabet. Chapter 5 does not follow the same pattern. Instead, it's chaotic and does not end with a simple conclusion, much like the suffering God's people were experiencing.

Lamentations helps see us that God welcomes our hard questions about sadness and suffering. It reminds us that it's okay to wonder why a good God allows hard things to happen. God invites us to share our emotions and frustrations with Him.

? *If Lamentations is poetry like the Wisdom writings are, why is it included in the Prophets?* Jeremiah (a prophet) likely brought this message from God to His people about coming exile by the Babylonians. Messages like these are considered prophecy, even though it's in the form of a poem.

WHO?	Likely Jeremiah
WHEN?	After 587/586 BC
WHERE?	Jerusalem
SUBGENRES	Poetry and personification
VERSE TO MEMORIZE	Lamentations 3:24

EZEKIEL

Major Prophet

Ezekiel was born into a family of priests and should have become a priest when he turned thirty. Instead, Babylon captured him in their first attack on Jerusalem. He turned thirty in a camp of exiled Israelites, far from the temple and city he loved. Ezekiel likely thought he would never become a priest, but eventually, God gave him a vision and allowed Ezekiel to serve as priest over Israel in the unlikeliest place: Babylon.

God called Ezekiel to do *sign acts*, or public actions, that taught the people who were watching. He had to do some crazy things—like chopping off his hair and burning it, lying on his side for 390 days, and only eating food cooked over animal poop.

God had a reason for asking Ezekiel to do those things: to show that God's judgment was coming for both Israel and the nations around them. Still, God continued to remind His people that He would give them new hearts through the work of His Spirit (chapter 34). God would (and does) bring new life to people who are spiritually dead. One day, there will be a new temple and a new city called "the Lord is there" (Ezekiel 48:35).

WHO?	Ezekiel
WHEN?	Sometime between 593–571 BC
WHERE?	Babylon
SUBGENRES	Poetry, apocalyptic, parable, and personification
VERSES TO MEMORIZE	Ezekiel 1:28; 36:26

DANIEL
Major Prophet

Daniel is a book that reminds God's people to hope in God. Even when they were exiled and living under the rule of another nation, God was still in charge. Daniel and his three friends, Shadrach, Meshach, and Abednego, were exiled after the attack on Jerusalem, just like Ezekiel was. Daniel and his friends were pressured to worship the kings of Babylon and to do the opposite of obeying God. Each time, they stood strong in their faith, and they were punished. Once, Daniel was thrown into a lions' den. Another time, his three friends were thrown into a fiery furnace. Each time, God honored their obedience and rescued them. God used Daniel and his friends to show that people can be faithful to God, even when obeying God could bring suffering or death. In every situation, God was in charge.

The book of Daniel is written in two languages. Chapter 1 is in Hebrew, chapters 2–7 are in Aramaic (the language of Babylon) and chapters 8–12 return to Hebrew. The break from Hebrew to Aramaic and back to Hebrew illustrates how God's people would return to their home. This book also includes dreams and visions that show how God is the true King who will reign forever.

WHO?	Daniel
WHEN?	Around 605 BC
WHERE?	Babylon
SUBGENRES	Narrative and apocalyptic
VERSE TO MEMORIZE	Daniel 6:27

THE MINOR PROPHETS

The twelve Minor Prophets are not less important than the Major Prophets. They are just shorter. Like God did with the messengers of the Major Prophets, God called a prophet to speak the hard truth about His judgment for unfaithfulness.

VERSES TO MEMORIZE:

Hosea 6:6	*Jonah 2:9*	*Zephaniah 3:17*
Joel 2:28–29	*Micah 6:8*	*Haggai 1:7*
Amos 5:24	*Nahum 1:2–3*	*Zechariah 9:9*
Obadiah 21	*Habakkuk 3:17*	*Malachi 3:6–7*

Minor Prophet	From	Sent to	Around When?
Hosea	Israel	Israel	786–746
Joel	Jerusalem	Judah	Likely between 539–331, but we don't know for sure
Amos	Tekoa in Judah	Israel (especially Samaria and Bethel)	760–750
Obadiah	Jerusalem	Edom, a nation south of Judah	Could be around 580 or later, around 840
Jonah	Gath-hepher, near Nazareth	Nineveh in Assyria	786–746
Micah	From Moresheth Gath but made his home in Jerusalem	Judah and Israel	735–710
Nahum	Elkosh in Judah	Nineveh	Possibly 640–621, but there is some disagreement
Habakkuk	Unknown	Only addresses God	608–598
Zephaniah	Jerusalem	Jerusalem	640–621
Haggai	Jerusalem	Jerusalem	Around 520 BC
Zechariah	Jerusalem	Jerusalem	520–514
Malachi	Jerusalem	Judah (Jerusalem)	500–450

Some details from the chart, such as approximate dates and locations, are taken from "The Prophets in History," *Holman Book of Biblical Charts, Maps, and Reconstructions* (Nashville: B&H Publishing Group, 1993), 62.

King	Did the People Respond?	Key Truth
Jeroboam II	No	God's love is faithful despite Israel's unfaithfulness.
Unknown	No	God's people should repent because the Day of the Lord (judgment) is coming.
Jeroboam II	No	God expects His people to act justly and pursue righteousness.
Unknown	No	God humbles prideful people to make His kingdom known.
Jeroboam II in Israel, Ashur-dan III in Assyria	Yes, but later they returned to their evil ways	God cares for all people, even those far from Him.
Jotham, Ahaz, Hezekiah	No	God asks his people to be humble, merciful, and just.
Manasseh	No	God's people can be encouraged that judgment comes to those who oppress them.
Unknown	Unclear	God is actively working in the world.
Josiah	No	God will bring justice forever at the Day of the Lord. Those who are humble can have hope.
Persian King Darius	Yes	God's temple is an important place because God dwells with His people there. Haggai wanted the people to rebuild it.
Persian King Darius	Yes	Faithfulness to God will bring about God's rule over everything.
Persian King Darius	No	God's people should honor Him.

THE GOSPELS AND ACTS

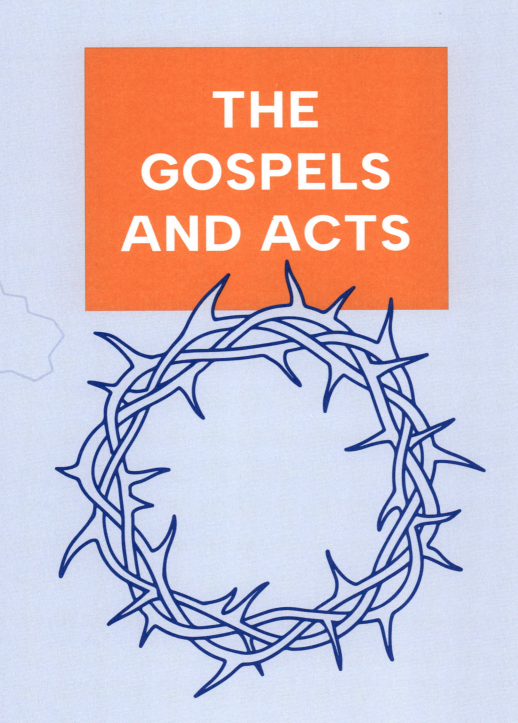

GENRE: THE GOSPELS AND ACTS

THE GOSPELS each tell the same story but in different ways. *Gospel* means good news, and the goal of the books is to tell the good news about Jesus's life, death, and resurrection. The Gospels include

- **Matthew**
- **Mark**
- **Luke**
- **John**

Each book was written by the person it was named after. While the Gospels are toward the end of the Bible, the story they tell is what every other book in God's Word points to. Jesus fulfills, or makes complete, the Old Testament covenants, which we read about in the Law. He is the promised Messiah who came to set up the new covenant—we read about it in the Prophets—with God's people. The Law, History, Wisdom, and Prophets all point to Jesus as the Savior. He is both God and man, and the only one able to make us right with God through His sacrifice.

ACTS is about the start of God's church. It includes Jesus's ascension, or when He went back to heaven, the Holy Spirit coming on the Day of Pentecost, and the start of many churches near and beyond where Jesus lived. During this time, Christians were mistreated, and some were killed because they had faith in Jesus. The good news about Jesus kept spreading anyway.

WHAT IS THE GOSPEL?

The type of writing of Matthew, Mark, Luke, and John is Gospel, but many Christians also refer to "the gospel." The gospel is the truth held within these books. Jesus lived a sinless life, died on the cross for our sins, rose again three days later, and ascended into heaven, where He talks with the Father for us. Everyone who trusts Jesus for salvation will be saved and will live with Him forever because of His great love.

In this book, the word *Gospel* will be capitalized when it means the genre of Scripture. When reading about the good news of Jesus, the word *gospel* will be lowercase.

SAME YET DIFFERENT

Matthew, Mark, and Luke are called the **Synoptic Gospels** because they share similar viewpoints that are specific but complement each other. John's book is not structured like the other three. Instead of focusing on Jesus's earthly ministry, John focuses on Jesus as God.

The four books share many of the same details and order of events. The Synoptic Gospels tell about Jesus's life event by event, although some events are not in the same order and some books leave out events. The goal of the gospels was to tell the good news of Jesus, highlighting what the author believed to be most important, not to provide an orderly list of events. None of the Gospel writers were trying to perfectly record the details of Jesus's life. That was not the goal. Instead, they told their stories in the order that would help them make the points they wanted to make.

- **Matthew** focuses on Jesus as King and the kingdom of heaven.
- **Mark** focuses on Jesus's miracles and how He fulfills Isaiah's prophecy of the Suffering Servant.
- **Luke** focuses on presenting the good news to both Jews (people born into Abraham's family) and Gentiles (people born outside of Abraham's family), showing how the gospel is for all people.
- **John** describes Jesus as the Word of God, the Lamb of God, and the Son of God.

PENTECOST

The Day of Pentecost is a major moment in the history of God's people. It was celebrated fifty days after Jesus's resurrection. When Jesus ascended, or was taken up, to heaven, He promised He wouldn't leave His people alone. He would send the Holy Spirit to help Christians do everything He commanded. On Pentecost, the Holy Spirit came to and started dwelling in everyone who followed Jesus. They began speaking in different languages about the good news of Jesus, and people around them who were far from home heard the gospel in their own languages. Followers of Jesus were sent out all over the world to share the good news. This is the day that the people experienced the Holy Spirit in a new way. He had always been among them, but because of Jesus's work on the cross, He would be *within* them, giving them power and boldness to tell others about Jesus. This same Holy Spirit also lives in you if you are a Christian. He gives you power, boldness, and the gifts you need to serve God.

SAUL OR PAUL?

In Acts we meet a man named Saul who tracked down Christians and threw them in jail. But God had big plans for Saul. Saul heard Jesus speak to him on the road to Damascus, and he immediately began to obey and worship Him.

Acts refers to this man as both Saul and Paul. However, his name is not changed like Abram's name to Abraham or Sarai's name to Sarah in Genesis. Saul is simply the Hebrew form of his name, and Paul is the Roman form. Paul spent a lot of time in Roman provinces, so he often went by Paul, but if he was in Hebrew-speaking areas, he'd still go by Saul. Paul, or Saul, became one of the boldest and most famous Christians in history.

WHERE ARE WE IN THE STORY?

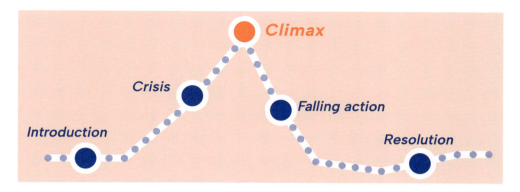

HOW TO READ THE GOSPELS AND ACTS

The Gospels and Acts take place at the most important moment in the story God has been writing through all of history—the climax. This is the moment that God's Son enters the world, experiencing life just as we do, but remaining perfectly obedient to God and dying on the cross so that we can have eternal life.

These five books are written as narratives, so read them as you would any story. Within these true stories are parables, or stories told to teach. It's important to remember that the writers are not trying to record everything that happened in Jesus's time on earth or every instance of the gospel being told to another people group in Acts. John tells us if everything was written down, "not even the world itself could contain the books that would be written" (John 21:25). There was and is too much to write!

The Gospels help us understand what that good news is; Acts reveals how that good news spread into all the world as the Holy Spirit gave God's people the power to share it and to trust God even when they were being mistreated. It's all about Jesus!

THE GOSPEL STORY IN THE GOSPELS AND ACTS

The good news is never clearer in the Bible than in these books. God the Son (Jesus) came to live with and among His people in a moment in time in ancient Israel. He is also with us today through the Holy Spirit. The Gospels and Acts show us a Savior who has come, not just to save us from sin, but to show us God so that we can know and love Him.

MAIN POINTS OF THE GOSPELS AND ACTS

1. Jesus is the Son of God, the Messiah that God promised in the Old Testament, who came to show God's love and offer salvation to both the Jew and the Gentile.

The Promised One for whom God's people had waited for so long had arrived. As John exclaimed, "Look, the Lamb of God, who takes away the sin of the world!" (John 1:29).

2. Jesus is bringing about the kingdom of God.

God's people demanded a king when God was to be their King (1 Samuel), but neither Saul nor any king who came after him could truly bring life and good to God's people. Only Jesus could do that. With the power of the Spirit inside God's people, they could do the mission of this kingdom, which is glorifying God and teaching the good news of Jesus (see Mark 1:15).

3. The Father and the Son have sent the Spirit to faithfully lead God's church.

The Spirit gives the power and skills needed to do God's will and reveal Him throughout the world.

KEY IMAGES

Water

Jesus offered living water to the Samaritan woman (John 4) and promised anyone who came to Him "will have streams of living water flow from deep within him" (John 7:37–39). Jesus used water as an illustration of the gift of trusting Him. Also, the Spirit is often illustrated by water in the Bible, so this water is a picture of the Spirit living inside the one who trusts Jesus. Jesus also was baptized in water as He began His ministry (Matthew 3:13–17).

Trees

In Genesis 3, Eve took fruit from a tree in the garden and gave it to Adam, bringing sin into the world as he ate what God told him not to eat. In the garden of Gethsemane, with large trees towering overhead, Jesus chose to be obedient to the Father, even to death on the cross. That cross, made from a tree, was where Jesus broke the curse that came from Adam eating from the tree in the garden of Eden (Galatians 3:13–14).

I AM STATEMENTS OF JESUS

In the Gospel of John, Jesus described Himself as "I Am," which is how God described Himself when He called to Moses from the burning bush (John 8:58; Exodus 3:14). Jesus also described Himself in the seven following ways:

1. I AM THE BREAD OF LIFE . . . . John 6:35–51
2. I AM THE LIGHT OF THE WORLD . . . . John 8:12
3. I AM THE GATE . . . . John 10:7–9
4. I AM THE GOOD SHEPHERD . . . . John 10:11–14
5. I AM THE RESURRECTION AND THE LIFE . . . . John 11:25
6. I AM THE WAY, THE TRUTH, AND THE LIFE . . . . John 14:6
7. I AM THE TRUE VINE . . . . John 15:1–8

WHERE WAS THIS HAPPENING & WHAT WAS GOING ON IN THE WORLD?

Jesus was born in ancient Israel, which is around the same place as modern-day Israel, when Augustus was emperor of the Roman Empire. Judea was under Roman rule, and Herod the Great was made king over Judea by the emperor. Herod was a cruel leader. When he heard that the promised Messiah had been born, he ordered soldiers to kill all baby boys under the age of two. (Matthew 2:16–18). Jesus's parents, Mary and Joseph, fled to Egypt with Jesus in His early years (Matthew 2:13–15).

Even though Rome ruled the area, the Jewish leaders of the synagogue still had a lot of power during Jesus's day. The temple priests worked with the Romans to maintain control over the people. The most powerful group of teachers were called Pharisees, and there were two other types, the Sadducees and the Essenes. Jesus's teachings seemed to rebel against the power of Rome and the religious leaders, which ultimately led these leaders to arrest and crucify Him.

THINGS YOU NEED TO KNOW

PROMISE FULFILLED

Matthew, Mark, Luke, and John wrote to help people understand that Jesus was fully God and fully man, as many were questioning this after Jesus went back to heaven. These Gospels show us that the Son of God came to earth and became man while also continuing to be God. He had every struggle of being human; He can understand every sad thing you face because He faced all the sad things during His life. Yet, He also lived the perfect life without sin and paid for our sins on the cross. He was the spotless sacrifice that the Old Testament Law required. He could only pay for sin in our place as humans and only be a perfectly acceptable sacrifice as the one holy God. He is both fully God and fully man.

TIMELINE OF JESUS'S LIFE

We don't know much about Jesus's life between His birth and the start of His ministry when He was baptized at the age of thirty. The Gospels record a lot about the last three years of Jesus's life as He chose disciples, taught about God, and performed miracles. Toward the end of each Gospel, the author zooms in on the last week of Jesus's life as He was arrested, tried before a court, crucified, buried, and raised to life again, before appearing to many and ascending to heaven.

PALESTINE IN NEW TESTAMENT TIMES

Below is a map of the area where Jesus traveled throughout His life.

KEY QUESTIONS TO ASK & ANSWER WHEN READING THE GOSPELS

1. What is the good news in this passage?
2. How is this passage showing that Jesus is both God and man?
3. How does this passage show God's great love for His people?

KEY QUESTIONS TO ASK & ANSWER WHEN READING ACTS

1. What does this passage show me is true about the Spirit?
2. How is God giving power to His people to take His gospel into all the world?
3. What does this passage teach me about what it means to follow Jesus?

PRACTICE IN THE GOSPELS AND ACTS

MATTHEW
238. Matthew 1:1–24
239. Matthew 3:1–17
240. Matthew 4:1–11
241. Matthew 5:1–20
242. Matthew 6:5–15
243. Matthew 8:1–34
244. Matthew 10:1–31
245. Matthew 13:1–23
246. Matthew 17:1–23
247. Matthew 21:1–17
248. Matthew 26:1–30
249. Matthew 26:36–75
250. Matthew 27:45–66
251. Matthew 28:1–20

MARK
252. Mark 1:1–20
253. Mark 2:1–12
254. Mark 6:30–56
255. Mark 9:33–50
256. Mark 10:1–31
257. Mark 11:1–11
258. Mark 12:1–27
259. Mark 14:32–52
260. Mark 15:1–41
261. Mark 16:1–20

LUKE
262. Luke 1:1–38
263. Luke 2:1–35
264. Luke 6:1–19
265. Luke 7:1–17
266. Luke 10:25–42
267. Luke 15:1–32
268. Luke 18:18–30
269. Luke 19:28–48
270. Luke 21:1–28
271. Luke 22:39–53
272. Luke 23:13–49
273. Luke 24:1–53

JOHN
274. John 1:1–18
275. John 2:1–12
276. John 3:1–21
277. John 4:1–26
278. John 5:1–23
279. John 6:16–58
280. John 10:1–21
281. John 11:1–48
282. John 12:37–50
283. John 14:1–31
284. John 18:28–40
285. John 19:16–42
286. John 20:1–31
287. John 21:1–25

ACTS
288. Acts 1:1–14
289. Acts 2:1–47
290. Acts 5:1–11
291. Acts 7:1–60
292. Acts 9:1–31
293. Acts 10:34–48
294. Acts 13:1–52
295. Acts 16:1–34
296. Acts 23:12–25
297. Acts 27:1–44

Passage: Luke 19:28–44

START-TO-STUDY

1. PRAY
2. READ AND REREAD

Date: Today

SUMMARIZE OR DRAW A PICTURE OF WHAT YOU READ:

Jesus came to Jerusalem on a small colt, or donkey, and people welcomed Him like He was in a parade.

---

3. ASK AND ANSWER *Review pages 17 & 18 for help with what to ask.*

ASK:
1. Why did Jesus ride a small donkey?
2. Why did the donkey need to be one that no one had ever sat on?
3. Why did the owners let Jesus's disciples take the donkey?
4. Where did the crowds come from, and how did they know He was coming?
5. How did they know Jesus was king?
6. Why did the Pharisees tell Jesus to tell the people to stop?
7. How could the stones cry out?

ANSWER:
1. Kings would ride in after war on majestic horses, but Jesus was humble, riding on a donkey instead.
2. Zechariah 9:9 said the promised King would come on a donkey. Maybe sitting on one that has never been ridden showed Jesus's power?
3. They don't say, but I don't think I would have.
4. I don't know, but it seems like they were ready and waiting.
5. They had heard about the miracles Jesus was doing in other places.
6. They didn't like that the people were worshiping Jesus as if He were God.
7. I don't know.

---

4. RESPOND AND PRAY *Write a prayer thanking God for what you learned about Him. Ask God to help you worship Him.*

God, thank You for giving me Jesus as my good, lowly, and humble King who came to bring peace with You. Thank You for all the many ways You bless us through Jesus! In Jesus's name, amen.

Passage: Luke 19:28-44

START-TO-STUDY
GO DEEPER

Date: Today

GENRE: Gospel

KEY QUESTIONS TO ASK AND ANSWER FOR THIS GENRE:

ASK:
1. What is the good news in this passage?
2. How is this passage showing that Jesus is both God and man?
3. How does this passage show God's great love for His people?

ANSWER:
1. Jesus is the humble, good King we need.
2. Jesus is worshiped as the Messiah that He is. He also told His disciples where the donkey was and just what to say so that they could borrow it.
3. Jesus entered Jerusalem just before He would be arrested and crucified. He knew what waited for Him in this city, but He came anyway, because He loves people so much. He knew the people shouting praise would later shout to have Barabbas released instead of Him, and He went anyway.

MAIN IDEA: Jesus is King over all.

KEY IMAGES: *Mark the ones that apply.*

MEMORIZE: Luke 19:38: Blessed is the King who comes in the name of the Lord. Peace in heaven and glory in the highest heaven!

ALL ABOUT THE GOSPELS AND ACTS

MATTHEW

The Gospel of Matthew was written for Jewish readers, so it includes many references to genealogies, or lists of families, and Old Testament passages. Matthew did this to help readers know Jesus's new covenant did not replace the old covenant. Instead, this new and better covenant fulfilled the Old Testament's covenant.

Matthew shows Jesus is the new and greater Moses, bringing His people out of slavery and giving them a new and better life. Jesus also is a King from the line of David, descended from Abraham. Yet He is not a king Israel would have recognized. He did not come with trumpet blasts but was born as a needy baby to a young mother. He is humble while also being in control of everything. Matthew wanted everyone to know Jesus was and is the promised Messiah of the Old Testament.

Matthew was a tax collector, and he includes more of Jesus's teachings on money than any other Gospel.

WHO?	Matthew
WHEN?	Around AD 50 or 60
WHERE?	From Bethlehem and Egypt to Galilee
SUBGENRES	Narrative, parables, and wisdom
VERSES TO MEMORIZE	Matthew 3:17; 4:4; 28:5–6; 28:19–20

MARK

The Gospel of Mark was likely the first Gospel written, as he collected stories and teachings from Peter, who discipled Mark. Mark was an evangelist—he traveled around telling people about Jesus.

His Gospel was written for Gentile believers in Rome, so he did not include as many details as Matthew did about how Jesus fulfilled the Old Testament promises of a Messiah. Rome was fascinated by great shows of power and scientific explanations. The Gospel of Mark focuses on Jesus's miracles, which only God can do. These miracles revealed Jesus could do things science could not explain, because He held the power of God.

This Gospel also focuses on Jesus's suffering, specifically as the Suffering Servant (Isaiah 52:13–53:12). Mark wanted all readers to know Jesus suffered so that we can have the opportunity to know Him.

WHO?	Mark
WHEN?	Mid- to late AD 50s
WHERE?	Bethlehem and Egypt to Galilee
SUBGENRES	Narrative, parables, and wisdom
VERSES TO MEMORIZE	Mark 2:10–11; 10:45

LUKE

Luke was a physician and was skilled in details. He traveled with Paul to tell people the good news about Jesus. He was likely asked by Theophilus, an important leader, to write an account of what happened with Jesus and the early church.

Luke wrote the book of Acts, and his Gospel and Acts should be read as a single story of Jesus and the launch of His church. Luke emphasizes Jesus's ascension into heaven in both books, making sure the reader knows it is a very important detail. Luke highlights Jesus's love for the lowly and Jesus's offer of salvation for the poor and the powerful, the Jew and the Gentile. Luke also includes more information from before Jesus's birth than any other Gospel. He includes details about Mary's meeting with Elizabeth, when the yet-to-be-born John the Baptist proclaimed Jesus as the promised Messiah by dancing in Elizabeth's womb.

Luke is considered a Synoptic Gospel, or one that is like Matthew and Mark. Like the other two, this Gospel includes the subgenres of parables, narrative, and wisdom. It also includes the songs of Mary and Zechariah.

WHO?	Luke
WHEN?	Between AD 58 and 60
WHERE?	Bethlehem and Egypt to Galilee
SUBGENRES	Narrative, parables, songs, and wisdom
VERSES TO MEMORIZE	Luke 2:14; 19:38; 24:44

JOHN

John, the author of this Gospel, was one of Jesus's closest earthly friends. He is known as the disciple Jesus loved. This book is very different from the other three Gospels, focusing mostly on the truth that Jesus is God's Son and what that means for His people. It does not contain early parts of Jesus's life but focuses on His ministry.

John shows Jesus as the Word of God, the Lamb of God, and the Son of God. He describes seven signs, or miracles, that make it clear that Jesus is God's Son, and he records Jesus's seven "I AM" statements (see page 115). Seven is a number often used to show completion. It seems John is showing that Jesus is God, who has power over everything. He is the Great I AM, one with God.

The seven signs in the Gospel of John include turning water into wine (John 2:1–12), healing an official's son (John 4:46–54), healing the sick (John 5:1–16), feeding the 5,000 (John 6:1–15), walking on water (John 6:16–21), healing a man who was born blind (John 9:1–12), and resurrecting Lazarus (John 11). Jesus did what no man could do, and He didn't just meet people's needs. He also forgave their sin.

WHO?	John
WHEN?	Between AD 85 and 95
WHERE?	Jerusalem, Judea, Samaria, and the surrounding areas
SUBGENRES	Narrative, parables, and wisdom
VERSES TO MEMORIZE	John 1:1; 1:14; 3:16–17; 14:6; 14:26

ACTS

Acts is the second half of Luke's story, and it records the history of the beginning of the church. It begins with Jesus's instructions to His people to go, make disciples of all nations through the power of the Holy Spirit, and His ascension into heaven. The Holy Spirit comes powerfully on the Day of Pentecost, appearing as tongues of fire upon God's people. These people shout the good news of Jesus in languages they don't know, through the power of the Holy Spirit.

The early church was heavily persecuted, or harmed, because they believed in Jesus. Many of Jesus's followers were even killed, but it did not stop the spread of the good news.

One of the people persecuting Jesus's followers, Saul, heard from Jesus and miraculously decided to follow Him. He traveled to places near and far alongside other believers, teaching the good news and starting churches. This Saul is also known as Paul, and he wrote many of the letters found in the rest of the New Testament.

WHO?	Luke
WHEN?	Between AD 58 and 60
WHERE?	Around the Mediterranean Sea and beyond, even into Europe and Asia
SUBGENRES	Narrative
VERSES TO MEMORIZE	Acts 1:8; 2:42

THE LETTERS

GENRE: THE LETTERS

THE LETTERS are messages written from a person, to people, at a real time, for a specific reason. They include 21 letters with 13 written by Paul:

- Romans
- 1 & 2 Corinthians
- Galatians
- Ephesians
- Philippians
- Colossians
- 1 & 2 Thessalonians
- 1 & 2 Timothy
- Titus
- Philemon

And there are letters written by others:

- Hebrews
- James
- 1 & 2 Peter
- 1–3 John
- Jude

Have you ever written a letter? Maybe you were telling someone "Thank you" for a gift or telling a friend about your life. During the time of the Letters, there were no phones, texts, or emails. The way people communicated if they weren't in the same place was often through letters. Letters were written by someone (or someone who had help) and delivered by another person, and that person often helped the person receiving the letter read and understand it.

Paul, James, Peter, Jude, and John (and whoever wrote Hebrews, because we don't know who that was) wrote letters to help churches and individual people live for Jesus. It had not been long since Jesus had been crucified and rose again, and the church had launched at Pentecost through the power of the Holy Spirit. Those who were present at Pentecost had gone out into all the world to share the good news about Jesus. They also set up churches as people in the places they visited started to believe.

These new churches were trying to figure out how to follow Jesus and be a church. The letters helped them know how to live, how to set up their church, and what they should avoid. Letters often address a specific situation, which we call an "occasion." These occasions could be disagreements or arguments within the church or lies about Jesus or Christianity that people in the church believed.

The issues the early church faced are some of the same issues we face today, and God helps us learn by reading these letters. They are God's inspired Word for the churches and people the Letters were originally written to, and they're for us as we learn to follow Jesus and live for Him through our lives and in our churches today.

WHERE ARE WE IN THE STORY?

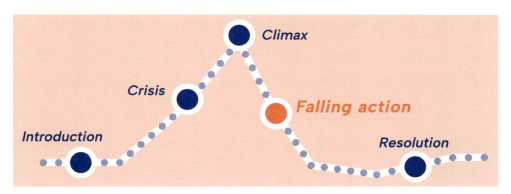

HOW TO READ THE LETTERS

The Letters often include a greeting, an expression of thanks, the body of the message, a list of quick instructions for how to live, and a closing. They often are written to answer specific questions, and many letters were likely responses to letters the writer received. Most letters address multiple issues within a church, so they can seem to jump from topic to topic. But for the church receiving them, the letters would read like instruction from a friend who knows them well and whom they know well.

Context

Letters are written to specific people, at particular times, in real places, so knowing as much as we can about what happened back then will help us better understand the main points of the letter now. We live a long time after these letters were written, but we can look for hints to help us learn what was going on. For example, if the writer talked about unity and asked the readers to avoid gossip or arguments, we know that the church was probably struggling with those things.

Occasion

The occasion of the letter is the reason it was written. Whatever the occasion is, it's usually easy to find—the author typically calls out the problem so that the people can solve it.

THE GOSPEL STORY IN THE LETTERS

The Letters proclaim the good news of the gospel. They also help readers understand how to believe it and avoid any false teaching that would lead them away from the true gospel: that our Savior, Jesus, lived the sinless life, died the death we deserved, and rose again, victorious over sin and death.

MAIN POINTS OF THE LETTERS

1. Jesus is the long-awaited Messiah who was crucified and raised from the dead.

In the early church, many people were still trying to figure out just who Jesus was and if all He said and taught was true. They also were trying to untangle their past beliefs from their new reality of following Jesus.

2. Don't listen to false teaching that points away from Christ.

The early church welcomed many preachers who traveled from church to church, but not all of them taught the truth. The writers of the Letters reminded God's people to love the truth and not be confused by these false teachers.

3. God wants the church to be led well and be unified, servant-minded, and worshipful of Jesus.

The Letters included instructions on the qualifications for leaders in the church, along with other instructions about being a church. The church is the clearest picture of heaven on earth, and God calls His church to look and act like Christ.

KEY IMAGES

Body

The Letters often describe the church as the body of Christ. Each person has a part to play, just like the body has many parts working together to make a whole person.

Fruit

The Letters use fruit or fruitfulness to describe the way people who follow Jesus live. They produce fruit like love, peace, joy, patience, kindness, goodness, faithfulness, gentleness, and self-control (Galatians 5:22–23). People will know if we are truly followers of Jesus by our fruit, or what they can see in our lives.

WHERE WAS THIS HAPPENING & WHAT WAS GOING ON IN THE WORLD?

The early church was persecuted, harmed, and even killed because they believed in Jesus. The disciples were hiding from persecutors when Jesus appeared to them after He rose from the dead. Acts also tells the story of the stoning of Stephen, along with others who faced hardship for their belief. These kinds of things were happening all over the Roman Empire in the time of the early church.

In AD 64 a great fire happened in Rome. This fire burned for many days and destroyed most of Rome. The leader at the time, Emperor Nero, blamed this fire on Christians. After this, their persecution became much more intense. Christians were often killed in public shows or even burned on stakes at night that everyone could see.

Around AD 66, the Jews in Jerusalem revolted against Rome, and around AD 70 the Jewish temple was destroyed by the Romans. Violence was commonplace, and so was pagan worship and large temples built to false gods. The Letters were written to encourage God's people living in a time of persecution, to help them make sense of suffering, to rebuke them for continued worship of false gods, and to teach them how they should live in light of the good news of Jesus.

THINGS YOU NEED TO KNOW

THE GOOD NEWS TRAVELS

The gospel was spreading into all the world, from the Middle East to the Mediterranean and beyond.

Find Jerusalem, Rome, Philippi, Ephesus, Corinth, Colossae, and Thessalonica on the map on the next page. Look at how far Paul traveled to take the gospel.

PAUL'S SECOND MISSIONARY JOURNEY

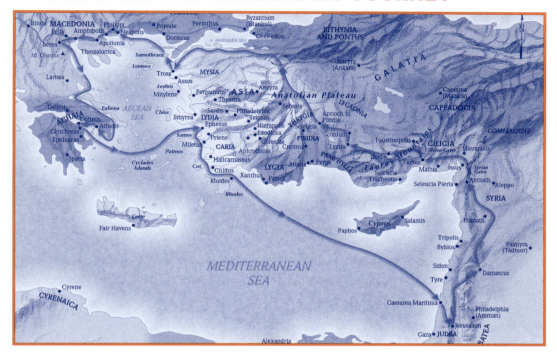

TIMELINE

Many of Paul's letters were written during the time recorded in Acts. As Paul traveled, he wrote to churches he had visited or started.

While the letters of Paul come before James in our Bible, James was likely the first New Testament letter written after Jesus's resurrection. James was Jesus's half-brother, and he was a key leader at the church in Jerusalem. Galatians, one of Paul's letters, was probably one of the first letters written, but scholars are not as sure about the exact time of its writing as they are about James.

DON'T MISS THIS: The book of James is similar to Wisdom literature, like the book of Proverbs. James knew God's people loved that book of wise sayings, so he shared the good news about Jesus and how His followers should live in a way that was familiar to them.

KEY QUESTIONS TO ASK & ANSWER WHEN READING THE LETTERS

1. Who is this letter from, and who is it to?
2. What problem is this passage of the letter addressing?
3. What does this passage say about how to live for Jesus?

PRACTICE IN THE LETTERS

ROMANS
298. Romans 1:1–17
299. Romans 3:9–26
300. Romans 5:1–21
301. Romans 6:1–23
302. Romans 8:1–39
303. Romans 10:1–13
304. Romans 12:1–21
305. Romans 15:7–33

1 CORINTHIANS
306. 1 Corinthians 1:10–31
307. 1 Corinthians 5:1–13
308. 1 Corinthians 8:1–13
309. 1 Corinthians 11:17–34
310. 1 Corinthians 12:1–30
311. 1 Corinthians 13:1–13
312. 1 Corinthians 15:12–34

2 CORINTHIANS
313. 2 Corinthians 1:1–24
314. 2 Corinthians 4:1–18
315. 2 Corinthians 5:1–21
316. 2 Corinthians 9:1–15

GALATIANS
317. Galatians 3:1–29
318. Galatians 4:21–31
319. Galatians 5:1–26

EPHESIANS
320. Ephesians 1:1–14
321. Ephesians 2:1–10
322. Ephesians 5:1–14
323. Ephesians 6:10–20

PHILIPPIANS
324. Philippians 1:21–30
325. Philippians 2:1–11
326. Philippians 1:1–14

COLOSSIANS
327. Colossians 1:9–23
328. Colossians 3:1–17

1 THESSALONIANS
329. 1 Thessalonians 2:1–20
330. 1 Thessalonians 4:1–18
331. 1 Thessalonians 5:1–11

2 THESSALONIANS
332. 2 Thessalonians 3:1–18

1 TIMOTHY
333. 1 Timothy 3:1–13
334. 1 Timothy 6:3–19

2 TIMOTHY
335. 2 Timothy 1:1–18
336. 2 Timothy 3:1–16

TITUS
337. Titus 3:1–10

PHILEMON
338. Philemon 1:1–25

HEBREWS
339. Hebrews 1:1–14
340. Hebrews 4:1–16
341. Hebrews 5:1–10
342. Hebrews 8:1–13
343. Hebrews 9:1–15
344. Hebrews 10:1–25
345. Hebrews 11:1–40
346. Hebrews 12:1–13

JAMES
347. James 1:1–27
348. James 3:1–12
349. James 5:1–11

1 PETER
350. 1 Peter 1:1–25
351. 1 Peter 4:1–11

2 PETER
352. 2 Peter 1:1–15
353. 2 Peter 3:1–18

1 JOHN
354. 1 John 3:1–24
355. 1 John 4:7–21

2 JOHN
356. 2 John 1:1–13

3 JOHN
357. 3 John 1:1–15

JUDE
358. Jude 1:1–24

Passage: Romans 5:12-21

START-TO-STUDY

Date: Today

1. PRAY
2. READ AND RERERAD

SUMMARIZE OR DRAW A PICTURE OF WHAT YOU READ:

Jesus is not like Adam. Adam brought death into the world with his disobedience, but Jesus brought life for all who will trust Him because of His obedience.

3. ASK AND ANSWER *Review pages 17 & 18 for help with what to ask.*

ASK:
1. Why is Jesus compared to Adam?
2. Why did sin have to come into the world?
3. What is a "type of the Coming One"?
4. Why are we all made sinners through Adam's sin?
5. If the Law "multiplies our sin," why did God give it to us?
6. What is the "gift of grace"?
7. What is condemnation?

ANSWER:
1. Adam was the first man, but Jesus was the first Son of God who would correct all of Adam's wrongs. Jesus reverses Adam's curse.
2. We don't know if sin had to come into the world, but we do know that God sent His Son so sin could be removed from the world when He returns.
3. A type is an example of something. Adam points to Jesus.
4. When sin entered the world, there was no way any of us would be able to avoid its power except Jesus. We inherited Adam's sin.
5. God is holy so we need to know what He requires to be holy, even though we can't do it.
6. The gift of grace is Jesus, the one who died on the cross for our sin.
7. This is guilt for our sin and our sin's need for punishment.

4. RESPOND AND PRAY *Write a prayer thanking God for what you learned about Him. Ask God to help you worship Him.*

God, thank You for sending Jesus when we were lost in our sin. Thank You for giving us the gift of grace through His death on the cross so that we can have eternal life! Thank You for Your love. In Jesus's name, amen.

Passage: Romans 5:12-21

START-TO-STUDY
GO DEEPER

Date: Today

GENRE: Letter

KEY QUESTIONS TO ASK AND ANSWER FOR THIS GENRE:

ASK:
1. Who is this letter from, and who is it to?
2. What problem is this passage of the letter addressing?
3. What does this passage say about how to live for Jesus?

ANSWER:
1. This letter is from Paul to the church in Rome.
2. Paul is helping the church in Rome understand what is true about Jesus and living life for Him.
3. We should live as those who have been set free from sin because of what Jesus has done! He has made us right with God!

MAIN IDEA: Jesus is better than Adam.

KEY IMAGES: Mark the ones that apply.

MEMORIZE: Romans 5:19: For just as through one man's disobedience the many were made sinners, so also through the one man's obedience the many will be made righteous.

139

LETTERS OF PAUL

Letter	When was it written?	Where was it written?	To
Romans	Likely around AD 55–58	Corinth	The church in Rome
1 Corinthians	Around AD 53 or 54	Ephesus	The church in Corinth
2 Corinthians	Around AD 56	Macedonia	The church in Corinth
Galatians	Around AD 48 or 49 (likely Paul's first letter, but the date is disputed)	Possibly Antioch	The church in Galatia
Ephesians	Around AD 60	A prison in Rome	The church in Ephesus
Philippians	Around AD 50s or early 60s	A prison in Rome	The church in Philippi
Colossians	Around AD 60	A prison in Rome	The church in Colossae
1 Thessalonians	Around AD 50–51	Corinth	The church in Thessalonica
2 Thessalonians	Around AD 50–51	Corinth	The church in Thessalonica
1 Timothy	Early to mid-AD 60s	Written between Paul's first imprisonment and his second	Timothy (about the church in Ephesus)
2 Timothy	Around AD 67	A prison in Rome	Timothy (about the church in Ephesus)
Titus	Likely early to mid- AD 60s	Nicopolis	Titus (about the church in Crete)
Philemon	Likely around AD 60 or 61	Likely from a prison in either Ephesus or Rome	Philemon (who lived in Colossae)

Reason	Key Themes
The Roman church was divided between Jews and Gentiles.	1. Rightness with God comes through Jesus alone. 2. The law can't condemn us anymore because Jesus fulfilled it perfectly.
This church was arguing. It was also in an immoral city, where people worshiped idols. Paul was reminding them to follow and worship the true God.	We run the race of life as faithful followers of Jesus.
Paul received a good report about the church from Titus. He was writing to encourage and teach them.	1. The new covenant unites (or connects) us to Jesus. 2. Suffering is part of being a Christian.
False teachers misled the church after Paul's visit, so Paul reminded the church at Galatia to not be deceived by false teachers, as well as to not be divided within the church.	We can't make ourselves right with God through our works. Being right with God comes from faith in Jesus and through life in the Spirit.
No clear reason. Paul sought to encourage the church to continue growing in their knowledge and love for God.	1. Christians can walk together in strength against spiritual warfare. 2. We can put everything under Jesus's authority.
Paul wrote to thank the church for their support and to remind them of the joy of life in Christ.	True unity and joy come from Jesus, and we can have it no matter our circumstances.
False teachers taught the church to doubt Jesus was really God.	1. Jesus is God and Lord of all. 2. Christians are made complete in Jesus.
Paul was responding to Timothy's report about Thessalonica and helping them grow in how to relate to others and how to think about Jesus's return.	1. Hope and peace in suffering come from Jesus. 2. We can point one another to Christ. 3. Christians wait on the future promise of resurrected life.
Paul wrote to give the church strength in persecution and to tell those who thought they had missed Jesus's return that they had not.	Stand firm while waiting for Jesus's return.
Paul wrote to correct false teaching and leaders who wanted to lead but were not qualified to do so.	God's people, the church, should try to avoid sin for God's glory.
Paul was nearing the end of his life and wanted to encourage Timothy to persevere and faithfully teach, even when it was difficult. He also combatted false teaching about Jesus's second coming already happening.	1. We can endure suffering because Jesus did. 2. We expect Jesus to come back because He said He would.
Titus was finishing the work Paul started in Crete. He needed to appoint elders for the church there.	1. Leaders in the church need God-given qualifications. 2. There is no greater gift than the gift of salvation and the Spirit.
Paul sent a personal letter (alongside his letter to the Colossians) to ask Philemon to grant freedom to his slave Onesimus.	1. The gospel changes everything. 2. Jesus has set us free from slavery to sin and called us to live a life of love toward others.

OTHER LETTERS

Letter	When and where was it written?	Who wrote it?	To
Hebrews	Possibly between AD 49 and 65; unknown location	Unknown	Persecuted Jewish Christians in Rome or possibly in Palestine
James	Around AD 45; Jerusalem	James, the brother of Jesus, and a key leader in the church at Jerusalem	Jewish Christians of the diaspora, or those who were outside of Jerusalem
1 Peter	Around AD 62–63; likely Rome (which he referred to as Babylon)	Simon Peter	Persecuted non-Jews
2 Peter	Around AD 64–66; likely Rome	Simon Peter	The churches in Asia Minor
1 John	Around AD 90–95; unknown; likely Ephesus	John, the son of Zebedee	Churches in and around Ephesus
2 John	Around AD 90–95; unknown, likely Ephesus	John, the son of Zebedee	"The chosen lady and her children," which could be a metaphor for the church or a specific family
3 John	Likely around AD 90; unknown, likely Ephesus	Unknown, possibly Ephesus John, the son of Zebedee	Gaius
Jude	Likely between AD 67 and 80; unknown location	Jude, likely the brother of Jesus, who came to faith after Jesus's resurrection (1 Corinthians 9:5)	General Christian audience or possibly Jewish Christians

Reason	Key Themes
Hebrews warned Jewish Christians not to go back to their old way of life under the Law.	1. Jesus fulfills the old covenant and is powerful over everything. 2. Jesus is better than any other way of life.
James told Christians they were not saved because of their works but that their good works would come out of true faith.	Don't just hear God's Word—do what it says.
Peter wrote to encourage the Gentiles while they were persecuted and struggling to stay hopeful.	God makes Gentiles part of His family and gives living, resurrected hope.
Peter addressed false teachings about Jesus's return and the coming judgment.	1. Knowing God's Word helps Christians avoid false teaching. 2. God calls His people to holiness.
John addressed false teaching that created doubt about God's promise of eternal life.	1. Love God and others. 2. God made Christians to be different from the world.
John addresses false teaching about who Jesus is and how we know God.	1. Jesus is God the Son, equal to God the Father and God the Spirit. 2. It is through God that Christians can love others. 3. Keep lying teachers out of the church.
John wrote to thank Gaius for welcoming good teachers like Demetrius and to ask him to rebuke Diotrephes, who was a false teacher.	1. Show hospitality toward believers. 2. The gospel is worth defending because it is true. 3. Christians can love others and love the truth.
Jude addressed false teaching that claimed special knowledge and taught freedom in Christ as being free to sin however you choose.	1. Remove false teaching quickly so that no one believes lies about the gospel. 2. Being a Christian doesn't mean freedom to sin; it means freedom from sin.

VERSES TO MEMORIZE FOR PAUL'S LETTERS:

Romans 3:23; 5:8; 5:19; 6:23; 10:13	1 Thessalonians 5:16–17
1 Corinthians 10:13; 12:27	2 Thessalonians 2:13
2 Corinthians 5:17	1 Timothy 2:5
Galatians 2:20; 5:22–23	2 Timothy 3:16
Ephesians 2:8–10; 6:10	Titus 3:5
Philippians 4:13; 4:19	Philemon 1:7
Colossians 1:15–16; 3:23	

VERSES TO MEMORIZE FOR OTHER LETTERS:

Hebrews 1:13; 4:12; 9:15	1 John 1:9
James 1:5	2 John 1:6
1 Peter 3:15	3 John 1:11
2 Peter 3:9	Jude 1:21

THE APOCALYPTIC WRITINGS

GENRE: APOCALYPTIC

THE APOCALYPTIC WRITINGS record God's dramatic actions that lead to the punishment of the wicked and the saving of the righteous, forever. Revelation is the only book that is wholly Apocalyptic, but other books of prophecy like Daniel, Isaiah, Ezekiel, Zechariah, and Joel have Apocalyptic writings in them as well.

SYMBOLS

Apocalyptic writings are a little like poetry. They use lots of symbols and word pictures. The writers do not explain what the symbols or word pictures mean, and the symbols get more challenging as the book goes on. Here are some symbols in Revelation:

- Jesus as a lamb, lion, or sun
- A dragon, beasts, and a woman in the sky
- Horsemen
- Seals
- Trumpets
- Lampstands
- Stars

Symbols are in every paragraph of Revelation! Many times, we can learn what the symbols mean because they refer to something from the Old Testament. But some are confusing.

NUMBERS

Apocalyptic writings also often use numbers as symbols. Revelation 1:4 says there are "seven spirits before his throne." But isn't there only one Spirit?

John is not saying there are seven Holy Spirits. He uses the number seven, which was considered a number of perfection, to show that what he is saying is complete or perfect. **The Spirit is**

perfect in every way, and His fullness is experienced around this throne.

Apocalyptic writings also mention time. These amounts of time are usually symbolic, not necessarily literal.

While Apocalyptic writing can feel difficult to understand or even a bit scary to imagine, it tells a story about a battle already won. It compares events on earth with events in heaven and reminds us that Satan will soon be defeated, Jesus will be celebrated as the King He is, and we will be with Him forever.

DON'T MISS THIS: While Apocalyptic writings can be confusing, they are much easier to understand when we are biblically literate (meaning, we know how to read the whole Bible). The more we study the whole Bible, the better we will be at understanding the confusing parts!

SOME OTHER APOCALYPTIC WRITINGS:

Isaiah 24–27	Joel 3:9–17
Isaiah 33–35	Daniel 7–12
Jeremiah 33:14–26	

WHERE ARE WE IN THE STORY?

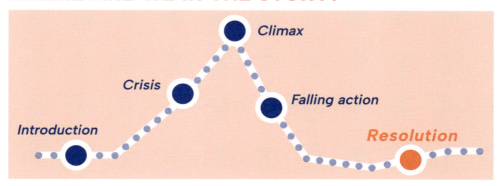

HOW TO READ THE APOCALYPTIC WRITINGS

Revelation and other Apocalyptic writings reveal how God's story ends. While the details aren't clear due to all the symbolism, this is clear: Jesus will return just as He promised, and He will judge everyone alive or dead. Jesus will put an end to all evil, sickness, sadness, and death. It's the best ending ever.

There are a lot of different ideas about what all the symbols mean. We should remember we can't know what the resolution of God's story will look like exactly. We should be slow to connect something in the writings to something happening in the world today, guess when Jesus will come back, or point to people or nations and say, "This is what Revelation is talking about!" We can't know any of that for sure. What we do know for sure is that Jesus will come back, and He will win the war against evil.

THE GOSPEL STORY IN THE APOCALYPTIC WRITINGS

Many people would point to Revelation 21 and 22 as the good news in Revelation. Jesus will return, and we will live with Him forever. That is absolutely the best news!

But there's also more good news throughout the book. God will hold evil accountable and will defeat Satan forever. The story will end in the exact way that He told us. We don't have to guess or worry. Instead, we can simply trust Jesus, knowing that He promised to return and that He never breaks His promises.

MAIN POINTS OF THE APOCALYPTIC WRITINGS

1. Jesus is the slain Lamb who returns as King, Judge, and Hero.

Jesus became the ultimate sacrifice for our sins. He paid for them on the cross and then rose again, defeating sin and death. Sin and death are already defeated. We are just waiting on the perfect Judge to return and remove sin and death from the earth forever.

2. Jesus will return to live with His people forever.

We do not have to wonder if Jesus will come back for us. God has never broken a single promise He has made in His Word! The best part of the new heaven and earth is not the streets of gold or the beauty of the jewels. The glory of heaven is that Jesus is there and that we get to be with Him forever.

3. The end is good for all who trust Jesus.

God has told us how the story ends, and it is a good ending for anyone who trusts in Jesus. God will do what He has said He will do, and He has promised good for those who love Him.

KEY IMAGES

Seals

The seals pictured in Revelation are like wax seals that must be broken for a letter or a scroll to be read. In Revelation, the seals seem to uncover God's plan for the end of the world and the beginning of the new heaven and new earth. Seven seals are mentioned in Revelation, a number that means complete or perfect.

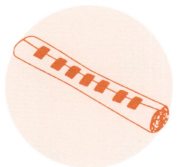

Water

Water continues to point to the way God purifies or cleans our hearts through the Holy Spirit (Revelation 1:15). Water points to the Spirit as the source of life throughout the Bible. It is not a mistake that the rivers flowing in the new heaven and new earth bring life to everyone (Revelation 22:1). People will know if we are truly followers of Jesus by our fruit, or what they can see in our lives.

WHERE WAS THIS HAPPENING & WHAT WAS GOING ON IN THE WORLD?

When Revelation was written, Christians were being persecuted first by Emperor Nero and later by Domitian, as well as the emperors and leaders between them. The emperors hated Christianity so much that they sent the apostle John to the island of Patmos, a place where criminals were sent. Many other Christians were harmed or even killed under these rulers. The other Apocalyptic writings were written around the time of exile. In both situations, it seemed like the end of the world was near. The Apocalyptic writings give hope to those who are suffering, because even if Jesus doesn't come today, He will return soon and make all things right.

THINGS YOU NEED TO KNOW

THE SEVEN CHURCHES

Revelation begins with letters to seven different churches:

1. Ephesus
2. Smyrna
3. Pergamum
4. Thyatira
5. Sardis
6. Philadelphia
7. Laodicea

Each letter evaluated the church's faithfulness to Jesus. Most did not receive good news, but Smyrna and Philadelphia were praised. They had remained faithful even in persecution or weakness. These seven churches were on a key trade route, so the letters would have gone from church to church. These letters aren't only for the seven churches. They are for every church. Every church should seek to be faithful, follow Jesus well, and avoid being like those who failed.

KEY QUESTIONS TO ASK & ANSWER WHEN READING APOCALYPTIC WRITING

1. What symbols are in this passage?
2. How does this passage—no matter how intense the images are—show the glory of God?
3. How or where do I see the goodness of God and His promise to save His people in this passage?

PRACTICE IN REVELATION

359. Revelation 1:1–20
360. Revelation 4:1–11
361. Revelation 5:1–14
362. Revelation 19:11–21
363. Revelation 20:1–15
364. Revelation 21:1–27
365. Revelation 22:1–21

Passage: Revelation 21:1-5; 22:1-5

START-TO-STUDY

Date: Today

1. **PRAY**
2. **READ AND REREAD**

SUMMARIZE OR DRAW A PICTURE OF WHAT YOU READ:

Jesus will return and make all things new.

---

3. ASK AND ANSWER *Review pages 17 & 18 for help with what to ask.*

ASK:	ANSWER:
1. Why is there a new heaven and new earth?	1. God is making all things new.
2. Why did the earth pass away?	2. The earth was broken by sin and needed to be renewed so that it isn't affected by sin anymore.
3. Why does Jerusalem look like a bride?	3. God uses the symbol of marriage to describe Jesus and the church. The Holy City (Jerusalem) is ready for God to dwell with His people there. It's beautiful.
4. Who is speaking from the throne?	4. It does not say, but it is probably God since He is on the throne in other places in this book.
5. What will it be like?	5. Amazing.
6. Who was He telling to write this down?	6. John.
7. Why is the river flowing from the throne of God?	7. The Bible uses water as a symbol of the Spirit a lot. God's presence is being seen and experienced through this flowing water.
8. What is the tree?	8. This tree is the tree of life mentioned in Genesis 1-2.
9. Why will there be no night?	9. Jesus is so bright that we won't need a sun. He will never leave, so the light will always shine.

4. RESPOND AND PRAY *Write a prayer thanking God for what you learned about Him. Ask God to help you worship Him.*

God, You've told us how the story ends, and it is good! Thank You for sending Jesus so that we can live forever with You. Thank You for promising to defeat sin, sadness, and death so that we won't have to experience those things anymore. We love You! We can't wait until You return to make all things new and to live with You forever. Help us to live by faith, able to withstand any hard time, because one day, the hard times will be over forever. In Jesus's name, amen.

Passage: Revelation 21:1-5; 22:1-5

START-TO-STUDY
GO DEEPER

Date: Today

GENRE: Apocalyptic

KEY QUESTIONS TO ASK AND ANSWER FOR THIS GENRE:

ASK:
1. What symbols are in this passage?
2. How does this passage—no matter how intense the images are—show the glory of God?
3. How do I see the goodness of God and His promises to save His people in this passage?

ANSWER:
1. A new heaven and earth, the Holy City coming down, the river, the tree, the twelve crops of fruit, the leaves of the tree for the healing of the nations.
2. The beautiful Holy City is coming down and is prepared for God, the loud voice booms from the throne, and the announcement that these words are trustworthy and true. These all show God's glory.
3. This passage shows the goodness of God in that He loves the world and us so much that He is making all things new. He is making it so that we can live with Him forever.

MAIN IDEA: Jesus is renewing all things. The new heaven and earth will be the best garden—even better than the garden of Eden. It is not just a garden, but a garden-city.

KEY IMAGES: Mark the ones that apply.

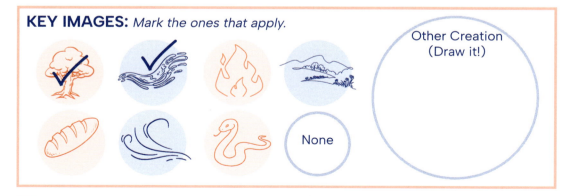

MEMORIZE: Revelation 21:3: Then I heard a loud voice from the throne: Look, God's dwelling is with humanity, and he will live with them. They will be his peoples, and God himself will be with them and will be their God.

ALL ABOUT REVELATION

In Revelation, the apostle John writes down the vision Jesus gave him while he was exiled on Patmos. John's writing has many symbols and events that are difficult to understand. But what we learn and know from this book is that God requires our faithfulness, Jesus will return to judge both the faithful and the wicked, and those who trust Jesus will not face condemnation but will be given eternal life.

Revelation includes more than four hundred connections to the Old Testament, making it the most connected book of the New Testament! Although we don't always see each connection, the early readers likely would have because they were familiar with the Old Testament and lived in the same cultural context.

God has promised to bless all who read the book of Revelation. Revelation 1:3 says, "Blessed is the one who reads aloud the words of this prophecy, and blessed are those who hear the words of this prophecy and keep what is written in it, because the time is near."

WHO?	John
WHEN?	Sometime between AD 90 and 95, but we don't know when the prophecies of the book will occur
WHERE?	Revelation was written on the island of Patmos. It references many cities in the Middle East and even the new heaven and the new earth that we will enjoy when Jesus returns.
SUBGENRES	Poetry
VERSES TO MEMORIZE	Revelation 1:8; 21:3–4

THROUGH THE BIBLE IN A YEAR
A 365-DAY READING PLAN FOR DAILY PRACTICE

Below you will find all the practice passages listed throughout this book. There are 365 passages, which can guide you through a year of reading the Bible. Keep using the four-step plan—Pray, Read and Reread, Ask and Answer, and Pray—as you read.

Read the FULL Bible in a Year

If you want to read the entire Bible in a year, read each day's assigned passage and whatever comes before the next day's assigned passage. So, instead of just reading Genesis 1 on the first day, you'll read Genesis 1 and 2, and then on day 2 you'll read Genesis 3–6.

Read the Bible in Two Years

To read the Bible in two years, alternate between reading the assigned passage and whatever comes before the next assigned passage. So, you'd read Genesis 1 on day 1, Genesis 2 on day 2, Genesis 3 on day 3, Genesis 4–6 on day 4, and so on.

Read the Bible in Three Years

To read the Bible in three years, space out the reading even more. You will read the assigned passage and then spend two days reading whatever comes before the next assigned passage. So, you'd read Genesis 1 on day 1, Genesis 2:1–14 on day 2, Genesis 2:15–25 on day 3, Genesis 3 on day 4, Genesis 4–5 on day 5, Genesis 6 on day 6, and Genesis 7:1–10, and 8:1–4 on day 7.

THE LAW

GENESIS
1. Genesis 1
2. Genesis 3
3. Genesis 7:1–10; 8:1–4
4. Genesis 9:1–17
5. Genesis 11:1–9
6. Genesis 12
7. Genesis 15
8. Genesis 21:1–7; 22:1–19
9. Genesis 28:10–22; 32:24–32
10. Genesis 37; 41–42

EXODUS
11. Exodus 1:1–14
12. Exodus 3:1–22
13. Exodus 6:2–13
14. Exodus 11–12
15. Exodus 14:5–31
16. Exodus 19:1–20:17
17. Exodus 25:1–9
18. Exodus 32:1–35
19. Exodus 33:12–23
20. Exodus 34:1–14

LEVITICUS
21. Leviticus 5:1–6
22. Leviticus 9:22–24
23. Leviticus 10:1–3
24. Leviticus 16:1–34
25. Leviticus 20:22–26
26. Leviticus 26:1–46

NUMBERS
27. Numbers 3:1–13
28. Numbers 3:40–51
29. Numbers 7:1–5, 89
30. Numbers 9:1–23
31. Numbers 13:1–33
32. Numbers 14:1–38
33. Numbers 16:1–35
34. Numbers 21:4–9

DEUTERONOMY
35. Deuteronomy 3:21–29
36. Deuteronomy 4:1–14
37. Deuteronomy 5:1–24
38. Deuteronomy 6:4–8
39. Deuteronomy 8:1–20
40. Deuteronomy 16:1–17
41. Deuteronomy 26:16–19
42. Deuteronomy 29:1–29
43. Deuteronomy 31:1–23
44. Deuteronomy 34:1–12

HISTORY

JOSHUA
45. Joshua 1:1–15
46. Joshua 2:1–21
47. Joshua 3:1–17
48. Joshua 5:13–15
49. Joshua 6:1–27
50. Joshua 10:7–15
51. Joshua 20:1–9
52. Joshua 24:1–33

JUDGES
53. Judges 2:1–19
54. Judges 3:12–29
55. Judges 4:1–24
56. Judges 6:11–40
57. Judges 10:6–18
58. Judges 16:1–31

RUTH
59. Ruth 1:8–17
60. Ruth 2:1–17
61. Ruth 2:18–23
62. Ruth 3:1–15
63. Ruth 4:1–22

1 SAMUEL
64. 1 Samuel 1:1–20
65. 1 Samuel 2:1–11
66. 1 Samuel 2:12–36
67. 1 Samuel 3:1–21
68. 1 Samuel 4:1–11
69. 1 Samuel 5:1–12
70. 1 Samuel 6:1–15
71. 1 Samuel 8:1–9; 19–20
72. 1 Samuel 9:1–9; 23–25
73. 1 Samuel 15:10–26
74. 1 Samuel 16:1–13
75. 1 Samuel 17:20–50
76. 1 Samuel 19:1–10
77. 1 Samuel 24:1–22

2 SAMUEL
78. 2 Samuel 5:1–5
79. 2 Samuel 6:1–22
80. 2 Samuel 7:1–17
81. 2 Samuel 11:1–27
82. 2 Samuel 12:1–25
83. 2 Samuel 22:1–51

1 KINGS
84. 1 Kings 3:1–28
85. 1 Kings 6:1–38
86. 1 Kings 8:1–21
87. 1 Kings 9:1–9
88. 1 Kings 11:1–13
89. 1 Kings 12:1–19
90. 1 Kings 17:8–24
91. 1 Kings 18:19–46
92. 1 Kings 19:1–18

2 KINGS
93. 2 Kings 2:1–25
94. 2 Kings 5:1–19
95. 2 Kings 12:1–21
96. 2 Kings 17:1–20
97. 2 Kings 22:1–13; 23:1–3
98. 2 Kings 25:1–21

1 CHRONICLES
99. 1 Chronicles 11:1–19
100. 1 Chronicles 14:8–17; 25–29
101. 1 Chronicles 16:1–36
102. 1 Chronicles 17:1–27
103. 1 Chronicles 28:1–21

2 CHRONICLES
104. 2 Chronicles 1:1–17
105. 2 Chronicles 5:1–14
106. 2 Chronicles 7:11–22
107. 2 Chronicles 29:1–36
108. 2 Chronicles 36:15–23

EZRA
109. Ezra 1:1–6
110. Ezra 3:1–13
111. Ezra 6:1–22
112. Ezra 10:1–17

NEHEMIAH
113. Nehemiah 1:1–10
114. Nehemiah 2:1–20
115. Nehemiah 4:1–23
116. Nehemiah 8:2–18
117. Nehemiah 9:1–36
118. Nehemiah 12:27–47

ESTHER
119. Esther 2:1–11, 16–18
120. Esther 2:19–23
121. Esther 3:5–15
122. Esther 5:1–14
123. Esther 7:1–10
124. Esther 8:1–9:2

WISDOM

JOB
125. Job 1:1–22
126. Job 2:1–13
127. Job 25:1–26:14
128. Job 28:1–28
129. Job 32:1–22
130. Job 37:1–24
131. Job 38:1–42
132. Job 42:1–17

PSALMS
133. Psalm 1
134. Psalm 23
135. Psalm 30
136. Psalm 37
137. Psalm 40
138. Psalm 46
139. Psalm 51
140. Psalm 62
141. Psalm 84
142. Psalm 91
143. Psalm 103
144. Psalm 106
145. Psalm 119
146. Psalm 121
147. Psalm 139

PROVERBS
148. Proverbs 1
149. Proverbs 2
150. Proverbs 3
151. Proverbs 4
152. Proverbs 9
153. Proverbs 10
154. Proverbs 15
155. Proverbs 21
156. Proverbs 27
157. Proverbs 31

ECCLESIASTES
158. Ecclesiastes 1:1–18
159. Ecclesiastes 3:1–22
160. Ecclesiastes 9:1–18
161. Ecclesiastes 12:1–14

SONG OF SONGS
162. Song of Songs 1:1–11
163. Song of Songs 3:1–11
164. Song of Songs 6:1–12

ISAIAH
165. Isaiah 6:1–13
166. Isaiah 9:1–7
167. Isaiah 11:1–16
168. Isaiah 24:1–23
169. Isaiah 30:18–26
170. Isaiah 35:1–10
171. Isaiah 43:1–28
172. Isaiah 53:1–12
173. Isaiah 61:1–11
174. Isaiah 65:17–25

JEREMIAH
175. Jeremiah 1:1–19
176. Jeremiah 9:1–16
177. Jeremiah 11:1–23
178. Jeremiah 13:1–11
179. Jeremiah 23:1–8
180. Jeremiah 29:4–20
181. Jeremiah 31:31–40
182. Jeremiah 36:16–32
183. Jeremiah 39:1–18
184. Jeremiah 50:17–32

LAMENTATIONS
185. Lamentations 1:1–22
186. Lamentations 3:1–24
187. Lamentations 5:1–22

EZEKIEL
188. Ezekiel 1:1–28
189. Ezekiel 2:1–9
190. Ezekiel 4:1–17
191. Ezekiel 6:1–14
192. Ezekiel 11:1–25
193. Ezekiel 20:1–20
194. Ezekiel 25:1–17
195. Ezekiel 34:1–30
196. Ezekiel 37:1–14
197. Ezekiel 40:1–4; 43:1–12
198. Ezekiel 47:1–12

DANIEL
199. Daniel 1:1–21
200. Daniel 2:1–30
201. Daniel 3:1–30
202. Daniel 5:1–31
203. Daniel 6:1–28
204. Daniel 9:1–19
205. Daniel 10:1–21

HOSEA
206. Hosea 1:1–11
207. Hosea 2:14–23
208. Hosea 6:1–11
209. Hosea 9:1–9
210. Hosea 11:1–12
211. Hosea 14:1–9

JOEL
212. Joel 1:1–15
213. Joel 2:12–32

AMOS
214. Amos 3:1–11
215. Amos 5:1–15
216. Amos 7:1–9
217. Amos 9:1–15

OBADIAH
218. Obadiah 1:1–21

JONAH
219. Jonah 1:1–17
220. Jonah 2:1–10
221. Jonah 3:1–10
222. Jonah 4:1–11

MICAH
223. Micah 2:1–13
224. Micah 3:1–12
225. Micah 7:8–12

NAHUM
226. Nahum 1:1–15

HABAKKUK
227. Habakkuk 1:1–17
228. Habakkuk 3:16–19

ZEPHANIAH
229. Zephaniah 1:1–18
230. Zephaniah 3:9–20

HAGGAI
231. Haggai 1:1–15
232. Haggai 2:1–23

ZECHARIAH
233. Zechariah 1:1–21
234. Zechariah 8:1–23
235. Zechariah 10:1–12
236. Zechariah 14:1–21

MALACHI
237. Malachi 4:1–6

GOSPELS AND ACTS

MATTHEW
238. Matthew 1:1–24
239. Matthew 3:1–17
240. Matthew 4:1–11
241. Matthew 5:1–20
242. Matthew 6:5–15
243. Matthew 8:1–34
244. Matthew 10:1–31
245. Matthew 13:1–23
246. Matthew 17:1–23
247. Matthew 21:1–17
248. Matthew 26:1–30
249. Matthew 26:36–75
250. Matthew 27:45–66
251. Matthew 28:1–20

MARK
252. Mark 1:1–20
253. Mark 2:1–12
254. Mark 6:30–56
255. Mark 9:33–50
256. Mark 10:1–31
257. Mark 11:1–11
258. Mark 12:1–27
259. Mark 14:32–52
260. Mark 15:1–41
261. Mark 16:1–20

LUKE
262. Luke 1:1–38
263. Luke 2:1–35
264. Luke 6:1–19
265. Luke 7:1–17
266. Luke 10:25–42
267. Luke 15:1–32
268. Luke 18:18–30
269. Luke 19:28–48
270. Luke 21:1–28
271. Luke 22:39–53
272. Luke 23:13–49
273. Luke 24:1–53

JOHN
274. John 1:1–18
275. John 2:1–12
276. John 3:1–21
277. John 4:1–26
278. John 5:1–23
279. John 6:16–58
280. John 10:1–21
281. John 11:1–48
282. John 12:37–50
283. John 14:1–31
284. John 18:28–40
285. John 19:16–42
286. John 20:1–31
287. John 21:1–25

ACTS
288. Acts 1:1–14
289. Acts 2:1–47
290. Acts 5:1–11
291. Acts 7:1–60
292. Acts 9:1–31
293. Acts 10:34–48
294. Acts 13:1–52
295. Acts 16:1–34
296. Acts 23:12–25
297. Acts 27:1–44

LETTERS

ROMANS
298. Romans 1:1–17
299. Romans 3:9–26
300. Romans 5:1–21
301. Romans 6:1–23
302. Romans 8:1–39
303. Romans 10:1–13
304. Romans 12:1–21
305. Romans 15:7–33

1 CORINTHIANS
306. 1 Corinthians 1:10–31
307. 1 Corinthians 5:1–13
308. 1 Corinthians 8:1–13
309. 1 Corinthians 11:17–34
310. 1 Corinthians 12:1–30
311. 1 Corinthians 13:1–13
312. 1 Corinthians 15:12–34

2 CORINTHIANS
313. 2 Corinthians 1:1–24
314. 2 Corinthians 4:1–18
315. 2 Corinthians 5:1–21
316. 2 Corinthians 9:1–15

GALATIANS
317. Galatians 3:1–29
318. Galatians 4:21–31
319. Galatians 5:1–26

EPHESIANS
320. Ephesians 1:1–14
321. Ephesians 2:1–10
322. Ephesians 5:1–14
323. Ephesians 6:10–20

PHILIPPIANS
324. Philippians 1:1–14
325. Philippians 1:21–30
326. Philippians 2:1–11

COLOSSIANS
327. Colossians 1:9–23
328. Colossians 3:1–17

1 THESSALONIANS
329. 1 Thessalonians 2:1–20
330. 1 Thessalonians 4:1–18
331. 1 Thessalonians 5:1–11

2 THESSALONIANS
332. 2 Thessalonians 3:1–18

1 TIMOTHY
333. 1 Timothy 3:1–13
334. 1 Timothy 6:3–19

2 TIMOTHY
335. 2 Timothy 1:1–18
336. 2 Timothy 3:1–16

TITUS
337. Titus 3:1–10

PHILEMON
338. Philemon 1:1–25

HEBREWS
339. Hebrews 1:1–14
340. Hebrews 4:1–16
341. Hebrews 5:1–10
342. Hebrews 8:1–13
343. Hebrews 9:1–15
344. Hebrews 10:1–25
345. Hebrews 11:1–40
346. Hebrews 12:1–13

JAMES
347. James 1:1–27
348. James 3:1–12
349. James 5:1–11

1 PETER
350. 1 Peter 1:1–25
351. 1 Peter 4:1–11

2 PETER
352. 2 Peter 1:1–15
353. 2 Peter 3:1–18

1 JOHN
354. 1 John 3:1–24
355. 1 John 4:7–21

2 JOHN
356. 2 John 1:1–13

3 JOHN
357. 3 John 1:1–15

JUDE
358. Jude 1:1–24

APOCALYPTIC

REVELATION
359. Revelation 1:1–20
360. Revelation 4:1–11
361. Revelation 5:1–14
362. Revelation 19:11–21
363. Revelation 20:1–15
364. Revelation 21:1–27
365. Revelation 22:1–21

MEMORY VERSES

Use the following memory verses as you read and study the Bible throughout the year. You might choose to memorize one per week, just picking your favorite fifty-two verses. Or you might choose to memorize two or more verses each week.

Leaders: If you are using this guide in a small group setting, you might choose to learn one verse together while encouraging students to learn another one at home during the week.

QUICK TIPS FOR MEMORIZING VERSES:

- Create motions for each word. Using your body to act out each word will increase focus and create "muscle memory" opportunities, where you remember a motion even when you can't remember the word.
- Write a song with the words or say them to a beat. A tune or beat will make the lyrics of the verse stick.
- Write it down multiple times. Writing with your hand helps your brain remember. You might even try writing down the first letter of each word.
- Say it in several silly accents. Repetition makes ideas stick, while changing the way you say it will keep your brain engaged and focused.
- Write the verse on a notecard and carry it with you everywhere. Review the card often.

1.	Genesis 1:1	10.	Numbers 14:18	19.	2 Kings 17:13
2.	Genesis 1:26–28	11.	Deuteronomy 6:4–6	20.	1 Chronicles 16:10–11
3.	Genesis 3:21	12.	Joshua 1:8–9	21.	2 Chronicles 7:14
4.	Genesis 12:1–3	13.	Joshua 24:15	22.	Ezra 3:11
5.	Exodus 3:14	14.	Judges 21:25	23.	Nehemiah 8:10
6.	Exodus 14:14	15.	Ruth 1:16–17	24.	Esther 4:14
7.	Exodus 20:1–2	16.	1 Samuel 15:22	25.	Job 23:12
8.	Leviticus 20:26	17.	2 Samuel 7:22	26.	Job 42:2
9.	Numbers 6:24–26	18.	1 Kings 8:23	27.	Psalm 1:1–2

28.	Psalm 27:4	54.	Malachi 3:6–7	80.	Galatians 5:22–23
29.	Psalm 56:3	55.	Matthew 3:17	81.	Ephesians 2:8–10
30.	Psalm 139:13–14	56.	Matthew 4:4	82.	Ephesians 6:10
31.	Proverbs 3:5–6	57.	Matthew 28:5–6	83.	Philippians 4:13
32.	Proverbs 16:24	58.	Matthew 28:19–20	84.	Philippians 4:19
33.	Ecclesiastes 3:11	59.	Mark 2:10–11	85.	Colossians 1:15–16
34.	Song of Songs 1:4	60.	Mark 10:45	86.	Colossians 3:23
35.	Isaiah 9:6	61.	Luke 2:14	87.	1 Thessalonians 5:16–17
36.	Isaiah 53:6	62.	Luke 19:38	88.	2 Thessalonians 2:13
37.	Jeremiah 1:7–8	63.	Luke 24:44	89.	1 Timothy 2:5
38.	Jeremiah 31:31–34	64.	John 1:1	90.	2 Timothy 3:16
39.	Lamentations 3:24	65.	John 1:14	91.	Titus 3:5
40.	Ezekiel 1:28	66.	John 3:16–17	92.	Philemon 1:7
41.	Ezekiel 36:26	67.	John 14:6	93.	Hebrews 1:3
42.	Daniel 6:27	68.	John 14:26	94.	Hebrews 4:12
43.	Hosea 6:6	69.	Acts 1:8	95.	Hebrews 9:15
44.	Joel 2:28–29	70.	Acts 2:42	96.	James 1:5
45.	Amos 5:24	71.	Romans 3:23	97.	1 Peter 3:15
46.	Obadiah 1:21	72.	Romans 5:8	98.	2 Peter 3:9
47.	Jonah 2:9	73.	Romans 5:19	99.	1 John 1:9
48.	Micah 6:8	74.	Romans 6:23	100.	2 John 1:6
49.	Nahum 1:2–3	75.	Romans 10:13	101.	3 John 1:11
50.	Habakkuk 3:18–19	76.	1 Corinthians 10:13	102.	Jude 1:21
51.	Zephaniah 3:17	77.	1 Corinthians 12:27	103.	Revelation 1:8
52.	Haggai 1:7	78.	2 Corinthians 5:17	104.	Revelation 21:3–4
53.	Zechariah 9:9	79.	Galatians 2:20		

FOR TEACHERS AND KIDS MINISTRY VOLUNTEERS
HOW TO USE THIS BOOK AT CHURCH

This book can be used in small groups, extended care at church, or even family devotionals every night. You might use it once a week, once a month, or when you are volunteering with a class of kids and have extra time.

In my local church, I teach the content in this book every week to second graders with the Fifty-Two Weeks through the Bible plan on page 168. Each week, I create a page for kids to draw a picture of the story and write down the big truth about God. This page gets included in kids' prayer journals.

Here's an idea of how to structure your time, based on how I lead my second graders:

1. **Write in prayer journals.** Kids may draw a picture, write what they'd like to pray for, or write or draw something they look forward to doing in the following week. Consider writing them a note after praying for their requests inside as well.

2. **Follow the steps to read the week's Bible passage.**
   a. Pray
   b. Read and reread
   c. Ask and answer
   d. Respond and pray

   Make the connections between key stories. Every important moment cannot be covered in fifty-two weeks, so bridge the gaps to help kids better understand the story God is telling in His Word. Here's how I'd tell it:

3. **Review the big story of Scripture and how each story points to Jesus.**
   a. Creation
   b. Fall
   c. Covenants
   d. Burning bush
   e. Out of Egypt
   f. Wilderness + the Law
   g. The Promised Land
   h. A cycle of obedience and disobedience
   i. Priests and kings
   j. Prophets
   k. Exile
   l. Return
   m. Jesus is born
   n. Jesus's ministry
   o. Jesus's crucifixion, resurrection, and ascension
   p. The launch of the church and its instruction
   q. Promised eternal life

4. **Learn a memory verse.**

5. **Pray for missionaries around the world** by choosing a country from an inflatable globe and looking up some facts about that area.

52 WEEKS THROUGH THE BIBLE

The 52-week plan on the following pages includes a passage, a theological truth about God, a memory verse, and a summary of what kids should understand by the end of your time together. Review each book's summary page for more help as you help kids understand the context of the passage within the broader story of the book.

1. The Good Creation: Genesis 1:1–31
God is the Creator.
Memory verse: Genesis 1:1
God created everything, and He created people male and female. It was all good.

2. Sin Enters God's Good Creation: Genesis 3:1–24
God seeks His people, even when they sin.
Memory verse: Genesis 3:21
Adam's sin brought many consequences. But still, God promised a Messiah would one day come who would crush the head of the serpent.

3. The Covenant: Genesis 12:1–9
God is our Covenant-Keeper.
Memory verse: Genesis 12:1–3
God called Abram to be a light to the nations and promised to bless the world through him. He would keep this promise in Jesus, who was descended from Abram and provides salvation to all nations.

4. The Call to Be Holy: Exodus 3:1–22
God is holy.
Memory verse: Exodus 3:14
God is unlike you or me. He is completely without sin and totally pure and right. When we know Him, He asks us to also be holy.

5. The Plagues: Exodus 12:29–42
God is powerful.
Memory verse: Exodus 14:14
God's great power is seen in the plagues and in the way He brought His people out of Egypt (from Exodus 7–15).

6. The Commandments: Exodus 19:16–20:17; Leviticus 19:1–4
God gives good instructions.
Memory verse: Exodus 20:1–2
God gave His people instructions as He set them up as a new nation. All these laws are both good and for people's good.

7. The Fearful Spies: Numbers 13:17–38; 14:6–10
God can be trusted, even when it seems impossible.
Memory verse: Numbers 14:18
The Israelite spies saw that the Promised Land was good. Everyone except Caleb and Joshua was too afraid to trust God would give it to them as He had promised.

8. God's Kindness: Deuteronomy 34:1–12
God is kind.
Memory verse: Deuteronomy 29:5
Even though Moses's sin caused him to die in the wilderness, God let him see Canaan.

9. God Goes with His People: Joshua 1:1–9; 3:1–17
God is with His people.
Memory verse: Joshua 1:8–9
God led His people into the Promised Land, but they didn't go alone. God went with them.

10. The Judges: Judges 16:1–31
God allows people to experience the consequences of their sin.
Memory verse: Judges 21:25
Samson was commanded to keep the Nazirite vow, but he did not obey. During this time, God's people did what was right in their own eyes.

11. The Faithful Redeemer: Ruth 4:1–17
God is our Redeemer.
Memory verse: Ruth 4:14
Ruth and Naomi faced the loss of their husbands, which meant they were without provision. God provided for them through Boaz, a distant family member.

12. The Prophet-Judge, Samuel: 1 Samuel 3:1–21
God speaks to His people.
Memory verse: 1 Samuel 16:7
God spoke to Samuel and gave him a message for the temple leaders. Samuel called them to repent. He also told God's people who God had chosen as king.

13. Saul, Israel's First King: 1 Samuel 15:1–35
God expects His people to obey Him, especially leaders.
Memory verse: 1 Samuel 15:22
Saul started off well but ended poorly. Saul wanted his own glory instead of God's. His time as king was limited, and God was disappointed by his actions.

14. David, Israel's Second King: 2 Samuel 7:1–29

God promises to provide a forever King.

Memory verse: 2 Samuel 7:22

David made a lot of bad decisions, but God was with him. Through the line of David and Solomon would one day come the forever King: Jesus.

15. Solomon, Israel's Third King: 1 Kings 8:1–30

God keeps His promises.

Memory verse: 1 Kings 8:23

Solomon completed the temple, where God's presence dwelled.

16. The Divided Kingdom: 2 Kings 17:6–23

God disciplines His people.

Memory verse: 2 Kings 17:13

Solomon misused his people, and his son Rehoboam was even worse. The people in the north did not want to be led by him anymore, so they divided the kingdom, with Israel in the north and Judah in the south. Each kingdom had kings, and most of these kings did not follow God. Their sin led to both kingdoms being conquered by other nations and exiled. God made it clear that He was the one exiling them.

17. The Exiles Go Home: Ezra 3:8–13

God gives His people favor.

Memory Verse: Ezra 3:11

After seventy years of exile, God gave His people favor. They were allowed to go home, rebuild the temple, and begin worshiping God there again.

18. The Law Is Read: Nehemiah 8:1–18

God gives great joy.

Memory verse: Nehemiah 8:10

Nehemiah worked to rebuild the walls and temple of Jerusalem alongside Ezra. When Ezra read the book of the Law to the people, they had great joy.

19. Esther Saves God's People: Esther 4:1–17

God protects His people.

Memory verse: Esther 4:14

Evil Haman plotted to destroy the Jews, but God placed Esther in the king's palace so that she could protect them.

20. God Speaks to Job: Job 38:1–18

God invites questions and frustrations, but He doesn't always explain why hard things happen.

Memory verse: Job 23:13

After losing everything Job loved, he continued to trust God. God did not tell Job why he faced hard times, but God was with Job.

21. The Righteous and the Wicked: Psalm 1
God's people delight in Him.
Memory verse: Psalm 1:1–2
This psalm reveals the life of the righteous and the wicked. It encourages people to choose wisely how they will live.

22. Seek Wisdom: Proverbs 3:1–18
God gives wisdom.
Memory verse: Proverbs 3:5–6
Proverbs reveals true wisdom, which only God can give.

23. Eternity in Our Hearts: Ecclesiastes 3:1–11
God has made us for eternity.
Memory verse: Ecclesiastes 3:11
Ecclesiastes reveals the frustrations of life and how purpose is only found in life with Christ.

24. By His Wounds: Isaiah 53:1–12
God promises to send a Savior.
Memory verse: Isaiah 53:6
Isaiah delivered difficult news about the coming exile and suffering, which took place by the time the book ended. God promised He would one day end suffering for good through Jesus. Prophecies about Jesus's coming are found throughout the Old Testament.

25. The Call of Jeremiah: Jeremiah 1:1–19
God calls prophets to deliver difficult messages of judgment.
Memory verse: Jeremiah 1:7–8
Jeremiah is known as the weeping prophet. The people did not repent in response to his warnings, and they were exiled. Jeremiah wrote Lamentations, a book of poems, to express his sadness over the people's lack of repentance and their exile.

26. A New Promise: Jeremiah 31:23–36
God forgives the sin of those who trust Jesus.
Memory verse: Jeremiah 31:33
Jeremiah both warned God's people of the exile and went into exile with them. God promised a New Covenant in His Son. It would bring forgiveness of sin and true knowledge of God.

27. The Spirit: Ezekiel 36:22–38
God promises to put His Spirit in His people.
Memory verse: Ezekiel 36:26
While exile was hard, God would not just bring His people home. He also would send Christ and His Spirit.

28. Daniel in the Lions' Den: Daniel 6:1–28
God rescues His people.
Memory verse: Daniel 6:27
Daniel was exiled to Babylon. The king passed a law against praying to God, but Daniel prayed anyway. He was thrown into a lions' den as punishment, and God rescued him.

29. Seek God and Live: Amos 5:4–27
God is just, punishing injustice.
Memory verse: Amos 5:24
The minor prophets call out the disobedience and injustice of both God's people and the surrounding nations.

30. The Reluctant Prophet: Jonah 1:1–17
God has great compassion for the rebellious.
Memory verse: Jonah 2:9
Jonah was not a prophet anyone should imitate. He ran from God and was swallowed by a big fish that took him closer to Nineveh. When people responded to his warnings by repenting, he got mad. But God loved Nineveh, too, not just Jonah and the Israelites. He welcomed their repentance and did not destroy them.

31. Splendor Like the Sunrise: Habakkuk 3:1–19
God is glorious.
Memory verse: Habakkuk 3:18–19
Habakkuk records a conversation between the prophet and God. In this final prayer, Habakkuk praises God for His glory as well as His justice.

32. The Word: John 1:1–14
Jesus is God come to dwell with His people.
Memory verse: John 1:14
Jesus is "God with us," and He is 100 percent God and 100 percent man. He has all power and all understanding about what it is like to be human like us.

33. Jesus Is Born: Luke 2:1–21
God brought peace on earth through Jesus.
Memory verse: Luke 2:14
Proclaimed by angels and seen by lowly shepherds, Jesus's birth was the most important event that almost no one knew about at the time. God came to earth!

34. Jesus Is Baptized: Matthew 3:1–17
Jesus is God's Son.
Memory verse: Matthew 3:17
In this moment, Father, Son, and Spirit are all mentioned. Jesus is prepared for ministry through this public declaration of Him being the Son of God.

35. Jesus Is Tempted: Matthew 4:1–11
Jesus was tempted as we are.
Memory verse: Matthew 4:4
Jesus fought temptation with Scripture, just as we can. He has been tempted like we are, but He never sinned.

36. Jesus Performs Miracles: Mark 2:1–11
Jesus has the miraculous power to both heal and forgive.
Memory verse: Mark 2:10–11
Jesus performed many miracles, proving He is God's Son, with power over everything. Jesus didn't just have power to heal or perform miracles; He had and has the power to forgive sin.

37. Bread of Life: John 6:25–40
Jesus sustains life.
Memory verse: John 6:35
In the book of John, Jesus describes Himself using seven "I AM" statements (review them on page 115). Only Jesus satisfies people's hungry souls.

38. The Entry into Jerusalem: Zechariah 9:9; Luke 19:28–44
Jesus is King!
Memory verse: Luke 19:38
Jesus is welcomed like a great king, yet He wasn't on a majestic horse. He rode a lowly donkey. Jesus is the King the people don't even know they need.

39. Jesus's Crucifixion and Resurrection: Matthew 27:45–56; 28:1–9
Jesus defeated sin and death on the cross, and He rose from the dead!
Memory verse: Matthew 28:5–6
This is the good news: Jesus lived the perfect sinless life, died for our sin in our place, and rose again victoriously. His actions prove He is Lord over everything and that He has made a way for us to be made right with God forever.

40. The Road to Emmaus: Luke 24:13–35
Jesus is alive!
Memory verse: John 14:6
Jesus explains God's Word to two disciples after His resurrection, showing them that He is alive. Today, Jesus helps us understand God's Word through His Spirit.

41. The Return to Heaven: Matthew 28:16–20; Acts 1:1–11
Jesus ascended to the Father.
Memory verse: Matthew 28:19–20
After Jesus appeared to many people, He ascended to heaven. This shows He won the battle against sin and death and finished the work He came to do. As Jesus moved from earth to His throne in heaven, it was like the coronation of a king. One day, He'll come back in the same way He went.

42. Pentecost: Acts 2:1–21, 42–47
The Spirit came, beginning the church.
Memory verse: Acts 2:42
The Spirit fell upon people, who spread the gospel to many listeners in their own languages. Many believed the good news! The church began, and God gave His people the power to be faithful even when it was very difficult.

43. The Calling of Saul: Acts 9:1–19
Jesus can transform lives.
Memory verse: 2 Corinthians 5:17
Jesus called Saul, who persecuted Christians, to follow Him and tell many people the good news.

44. Paul and Silas in Jail: Acts 16:22–34
God gives His people power to share the good news.
Memory verse: Acts 1:8
Paul faced jail, shipwrecks, a snakebite, and more. Everywhere he went, God showed the good news about Jesus through him.

45. Adam and Jesus: Romans 5:12–21
Jesus is the second Adam.
Memory verse: Romans 5:19
Paul wrote many letters to churches he helped begin or had visited. In this passage from Romans, Paul highlights Jesus as the better Adam. Adam was disobedient when Jesus was perfectly obedient. Adam brought a curse while Jesus reversed the curse and brought a blessing. Adam brought death, but Jesus brought life.

46. The Body of Christ: 1 Corinthians 12:12–27
God gives His people good gifts to use for the church.
Memory verse: 1 Corinthians 12:27
Each person in the church has an important role (even kids)!

47. The Fruit of Spirit: Galatians 5:16–26
God's people are different from the world because the Spirit creates fruit.
Memory verse: Galatians 5:22–23
What do Christians look like? They look like the description in Galatians 5:22–23. Christians can pray and ask the Spirit to make this fruit grow in their lives.

48. The Armor of God: Ephesians 6:10–19
God gives His people every tool they need to live for Him.
Memory verse: Ephesians 6:10
Each piece of armor is important for the believer. None of it can be left at home!

49. Being Content Anywhere: Philippians 4:10–20
God meets His people's needs.
Memory verse: Philippians 4:19
Paul wrote Philippians from prison, and yet, he could still say he was content with what God had given him.

50. The New Covenant: Hebrews 9:1–15
Jesus fulfills the Old Testament.
Memory verse: Hebrews 9:15
Hebrews points back to the Old Testament, consistently showing that Jesus has brought a better covenant through His blood. Jesus is the better priest, serving in the better tabernacle. Only His blood could save God's people forever.

51. Tame the Tongue: James 3:1–18
God gives wisdom for how to live.
Memory verse: James 3:13
God cares about how His people talk and live. He describes how to live for Him in His Word.

52. A Day Is Coming: Revelation 21:1–5; 22:1–5
Jesus will return and make all things new and right.
Memory verse: Revelation 21:3
Jesus will do just as He promised. He will return and there will be no more sickness, sadness, death, or sin. His people will live with Him forever!